W9-BTD-437

"Liv," He Called Softly, But She Didn't Budge.

Apparently she was more tired than she'd realized. He found a spare blanket in the closet, and walked back to the bed to cover her. For reasons he couldn't begin to understand, he felt compelled to just look at her.

She's not your type, he reminded himself.

If he was going to be honest with himself, his "type" had plenty to offer physically, but intellectually, he was usually left feeling bored and unfulfilled. Maybe it was time for a change of pace.

Seducing a woman like Liv might be just what he needed to spice things up.

NORTH AUSTIN BRANCH
5724 W. NORTH AVE,
CHICAGO, IL 60639

Dear Reader,

Welcome to the next installment of my ROYAL SEDUCTIONS series. I can hardly believe we're already on book six, the story of Prince Aaron Felix Gastel Alexander and genetic botanist Olivia Montgomery. A royal heir and an orphan abandoned at the age of three.

Can you say, opposites attract?

These two were definitely a handful! How do you take two independent, headstrong people and make them bend to your creative will? The truth is, you don't. As a writer, all you can really do is sit back and let them lead you on their journey. And with Aaron and Liv, there was never a dull moment. Especially when these two very different people suddenly realized maybe they weren't so different after all. And when all is said and done, family isn't about bloodlines and pedigrees and fitting in, but instead the people you hold most dear in your heart.

In July don't forget to look for the next book in the ROYAL SEDUCTIONS series, the story of Princess Louisa and millionaire mogul Garrett Sutherland.

Best,

Michelle

MICHELLE CELMER

CHRISTMAS WITH THE PRINCE

Published by Silhouette Books
America's Publisher of Contemporary Romance

If you purchased this book without a cover you should be aware that this book is stolen property. It was reported as "unsold and destroyed" to the publisher, and neither the author nor the publisher has received any payment for this "stripped book."

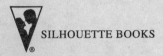

SILHOUETTE BOOKS

ISBN-13: 978-0-373-76979-7

Recycling programs for this product may not exist in your area.

CHRISTMAS WITH THE PRINCE

Copyright © 2009 by Michelle Celmer

All rights reserved. Except for use in any review, the reproduction or utilization of this work in whole or in part in any form by any electronic, mechanical or other means, now known or hereafter invented, including xerography, photocopying and recording, or in any information storage or retrieval system, is forbidden without the written permission of the editorial office, Silhouette Books, 233 Broadway, New York, NY 10279 U.S.A.

This is a work of fiction. Names, characters, places and incidents are either the product of the author's imagination or are used fictitiously, and any resemblance to actual persons, living or dead, business establishments, events or locales is entirely coincidental.

This edition published by arrangement with Harlequin Books S.A.

® and TM are trademarks of Harlequin Books S.A., used under license. Trademarks indicated with ® are registered in the United States Patent and Trademark Office, the Canadian Trade Marks Office and in other countries.

Visit Silhouette Books at www.eHarlequin.com

Printed in U.S.A.

R0422776621

Books by Michelle Celmer

Silhouette Desire

NORTH AUSTIN BRANCH
5724 W. NORTH AVE,
CHICAGO, IL 60639

Playing by the Baby Rules #1566
The Seduction Request #1626
Bedroom Secrets #1656
Round-the-Clock Temptation #1683
House Calls #1703
The Millionaire's Pregnant Mistress #1739
The Secretary's Secret #1774
Best Man's Conquest #1799
*The King's Convenient Bride #1876
*The Illegitimate Prince's Baby #1877
*An Affair with the Princess #1900
*The Duke's Boardroom Affair #1919
*Royal Seducer #1951
The Oilman's Baby Bargain #1970
*Christmas with the Prince #1979

*Royal Seductions

MICHELLE CELMER

Bestselling author Michelle Celmer lives in southeastern Michigan with her husband, their three children, two dogs and two cats. When she's not writing or busy being a mom, you can find her in the garden or curled up with a romance novel. And if you twist her arm real hard you can usually persuade her into a day of power shopping.

Michelle loves to hear from readers. Visit her Web site at www.michellecelmer.com, or write her at P.O. Box 300, Clawson, MI 48017.

To my mom,
who has been not only my teacher, my confidant,
and my most dedicated fan, but one of my best friends.

Love you!

One

Olivia Montgomery was attractive for a scientist.

Attractive in a brainy, geeky sort of way. From a distance, at least. And not at all what Prince Aaron had expected.

He watched her gaze up at the castle from his office window, a look of awe on her heart-shaped face, her bow mouth formed into a perfect *O* beneath eyes as large as dinner plates.

He supposed it wasn't every day that a woman was asked to uproot her entire life, stay at a royal castle for an indeterminable period and use her vast knowledge to save an entire country from potential absolute financial devastation.

Of course, from what he'd read of their new guest, her life to date had been anything but typical. Most kids didn't graduate from high school at fifteen, receive their Ph.D. at twenty-two and earn a reputation as a pioneer in the field of botanical genetics at twenty-four. He would swear she didn't look a day over eighteen, due in part to the long, blondish-brown hair she wore pulled back in a ponytail and the backpack she carried slung over one shoulder.

He watched as Derek, his personal assistant, led her into the castle, then he took a seat at his desk to wait for them, feeling uncharacteristically anxious. He had been assured that in the field of genetic botany, she was the best. Meaning she could very well be their last hope.

Specialist after specialist had been unable to diagnose or effectively treat the blight plaguing their crops. A disease that had begun in the east fields, and spread to affect not only a good portion of the royal family's land, but had recently been reported in surrounding farms, as well. Unchecked, the effects could be financially devastating to their agriculturally based economy.

His family—hell, the entire country—was counting on him to find a way to fix it.

Talk about pressure. He used to believe that his older brother, Christian, the crown prince, had it rough, carrying the burden of one day taking over as ruler, and the responsibility of marrying and producing a royal heir. But to Aaron's surprise, after a slightly rocky start, Chris seemed to be embracing his new title as husband.

For Aaron, the thought of tying himself down to one woman for the rest of his life gave him cold chills. Not that he didn't love women. He just loved lots of different women. And when the novelty of one wore thin, he liked having the option of moving on to something new. Although, now that Chris was blissfully married off, their mother, the queen, had taken an active and unsettling interest in Aaron's love life. He never knew there were so many eligible young women with royal blood, and his mother seemed hell-bent on setting him up with every single one of them.

She would figure out eventually that all the meddling in the world wouldn't bring him any closer to the altar. At least, he hoped she would. She could instead focus on marrying off his twin sisters, Anne and Louisa.

Several minutes passed before there was a rap at Aaron's office door. Undoubtedly Derek had been explaining policy for meeting members of the royal family to their guest. What she should and shouldn't do or say. It could be a bit overwhelming. Especially for someone who had never been in the presence of royalty before.

"Come in," he called.

The door opened and Derek appeared, followed

closely by Miss Montgomery. Aaron rose from his chair to greet her, noticing right away her height. He was just over six feet tall, and in flat-heeled, conservative loafers she stood nearly eye level. It was difficult to see her figure under the loose khaki pants and baggy, cable-knit sweater, although she gave the impression of being quite slim. *Too* slim, even. All sharp and angular.

Missing was the lab coat, pocket protector and cola-bottle glasses one might expect from a scientist. She wore no makeup or jewelry, and was for all accounts quite plain, yet she was undeniably female. Attractive in a simple way. Cute and girlish. Although at twenty-five, she was definitely a woman.

"Your Highness," Derek said, "May I introduce Miss Olivia Montgomery, of the United States." He turned to Miss Montgomery. "Miss Montgomery, may I present Prince Aaron Felix Gastel Alexander of Thomas Isle."

Miss Montgomery stuck her hand out to shake his, then, realizing her error, snatched it back and dipped into an awkward, slightly wobbly curtsy instead, her cheeks coloring an enchanting shade of pink. "It's an honor to be here, sir—I mean, Your Highness."

Her voice was softer than he'd expected. Low and breathy, and dare he say a little sexy. He'd always found an American accent undeniably appealing.

"The honor is mine," he said, reaching out for a shake. She hesitated a second, then accepted his hand. Her hands were slender and fine-boned, with long fingers that wrapped around his with a surprisingly firm grip. Her skin was warm and soft, her nails short but neatly filed.

She gazed at him with eyes an intriguing shade—not quite brown, and not quite green—and so large and inquisitive they seemed to take up half her face. Everything about her was a little overexaggerated and…unexpected.

But she couldn't be any less his type. He preferred his women small and soft in all the right places, and the more beautiful the better. Not particularly smart, either, because frankly, he wasn't in it for the conversation. The fewer brains, the less likely he was to become attached. As long as she could navigate a golf course or squash court, or rock a pair of cross-country skis. Sailing experience was a plus, as well, and if she could climb a rock wall, he would be in sheer heaven.

Somehow he didn't see Miss Montgomery as the athletic type.

"I'll be in my office if you need me, sir," Derek told him, then slipped out of the room, closing the door behind him. As it snapped shut, he could swear he saw Miss Montgomery flinch.

He gestured to the chair opposite his desk. "Miss Montgomery, make yourself comfortable."

She set her backpack on the floor beside her and sat awkwardly on the very edge of the cushion. She folded her hands in her lap, then unfolded them. Then she tucked them around the sides of her thighs and under her legs. She looked very *un*comfortable.

"I apologize for being so late," she said.

He perched on the corner of his desk. "I hear you hit some bad weather on the way over."

She nodded. "It was a bumpy flight. And I'm not real crazy about flying to begin with. In fact, I might look into taking a ship home."

"Can I offer you a drink, Miss Montgomery?"

"No, thank you. And please, call me Liv. Everyone does."

"All right, Liv. And because we'll be spending quite some time together, you should call me Aaron."

She hesitated, then asked, "Is that…allowed?"

He grinned. "I assure you, it's perfectly acceptable."

She nodded, her head a little wobbly on the end of a very long and slender neck. She had the kind of throat made for stroking and nibbling. But somehow he didn't see her as the nibbling type. She had shy and repressed written all over her. No doubt, he could teach her a thing or two. Not that he intended to. Or even possessed the desire.

Well, maybe just a little, but purely out of curiosity.

"My family apologizes that they couldn't be here to greet you," he told her. "They're in England to see my father's cardiologist. They'll be back Friday."

"I look forward to meeting them," she said, although she sounded more wary than enthusiastic.

She had no reason to be apprehensive. In the history of his father's reign as king, her visit might very well be the most anticipated and appreciated. Not that she was offering her services for free. They had agreed to make a handsome donation to fund her research. Personally she hadn't asked for anything more than room and board. No special amenities, or even a personal maid to tend to her care.

"I'm told that you looked at the disease samples we sent you," he said.

She nodded, not so wobbly this time. "I did. As well as the data from the other specialists."

"And what conclusion have you drawn?"

"You have yourself a very unusual, very resistant strain of disease that I've never seen before. And trust me when I say I've pretty much seen them all."

"Your references are quite impressive. I've been assured that if anyone can diagnose the problem, it's you."

"There is no *if.*" She looked him directly in the eye and said firmly, "It's simply a matter of *when.*"

Her confidence, and the forceful tone with which she spoke, nearly knocked him backward.

Well, he hadn't seen that coming. It was almost as though someone flipped a switch inside of her and a completely different woman emerged. She sat a little straighter and her voice sounded stronger. Just like that, he gained an entirely new level of respect for her.

"Have you thought about my suggestion to stop all agricultural exports?" she asked.

That was *all* he'd been thinking about. "Even the unaffected crops?"

"I'm afraid so."

"Is that really necessary?"

"For all we know, it could be lying dormant in the soil of areas that *appear* unaffected. And until we know what this thing is, we don't want it to get off the island."

He knew she was right, but the financial repercussions would sting. "That means we have only until the next season, less than five months, to identify the disease and find an environmentally friendly cure."

Environmentally friendly so that they could maintain their reputation as a totally organic, green island. Millions had been spent to radically alter the way every farmer grew his crops. It was what set them apart from other distributors and made them a valuable commodity.

"Can it be done in that time frame?" he asked.

"The truth is, I don't know. These things can take time."

It wasn't what he wanted to hear, but he appreciated her honesty. He'd wanted her to fly in, have the problem solved in a week or two, then be on her way, making him look like a hero in not only his family, but also his country's eyes.

So much for that delusion of grandeur.

"Once I get set up in the lab and have a few days to study the rest of the data, I may be able to give you some sort of time frame," she said.

"We have a student from the university on standby, should you need an assistant."

"I'll need someone to take samples, but in the lab I prefer to work alone. You have all the equipment I need?"

"Everything on your list." He rose to his feet. "I can show you to your room and give you time to settle in."

She stood, as well, smoothing the front of her slacks with her palms. He couldn't help wondering what she was hiding behind that bulky sweater. Were those breasts he saw? And hips? Maybe she wasn't as sharp and angular as he'd first thought.

"If you don't mind," she said, "I'd rather get right to work."

He gestured to the door. "Of course. I'll take you right to the lab."

She certainly didn't waste any time, did she? And he was relieved to know that she seemed determined to help.

The sooner they cured this blight, the sooner they could all breathe easy again.

Two

Liv followed her host through the castle, heart thumping like mad, praying she didn't do something stupid like trip over her own feet and fall flat on her face.

Prince Aaron was, by far, the most beautiful man she had ever laid eyes on. His hair so dark and soft-looking, his eyes a striking, mesmerizing shade of green, his full lips always turned up in a sexy smile.

He had the deep and smoky voice of a radio DJ and a body to die for. A muscular backside under dark tailored slacks. Wide shoulders and bulging pecs encased in midnight-blue cashmere. As she followed him through the castle she felt hypnotized by the fluid grace with which he moved.

He was…perfect. An eleven on a scale of one to

ten. And the antithesis of the scientists and geeks she was used to keeping company with. Like William, her fiancé—or at least he would be her fiancé if she decided to accept the proposal of marriage he had stunned her with just last night in the lab.

Fifteen years her senior and her mentor since college, Will wasn't especially handsome, and he was more studious than sexy, but he was kind and sweet and generous. The truth was, his proposal had come so far out of left field that it had nearly given her whiplash. They had never so much as kissed, other than a friendly peck on the cheek on holidays or special occasions. But she respected him immensely and loved him as a friend. So she had promised to give his proposal serious thought while she was away. Even though, when he'd kissed her goodbye at the airport—a real kiss with lips and tongue—she hadn't exactly seen fireworks. But sexual attraction was overrated and fleeting at best. They had respect and a deep sense of friendship.

Although she couldn't help wondering if she would be settling.

Yeah, right. Like she had a mob of other men pounding down her door. She couldn't even recall the last time she'd been on a date. And sex, well, it had been so long she wasn't sure she even remembered how. Not that it had been smoking hot anyhow. The one man she'd slept with in college had been a budding nuclear physicist, and more concerned with mathematical equations than figuring out sexual complexities. She bet Prince Aaron knew his way around a woman's body.

Right, Liv, and I suppose the prince is going to show you.

The thought was so ridiculous she nearly laughed out loud. What would a gorgeous, sexy prince see in a nerdy, totally *unsexy* woman like her?

"So, what do you think of our island?" Aaron asked as they descended the stairs together.

"What I've seen of it is beautiful. And the castle isn't at all what I expected."

"What did you expect?"

"Honestly, I thought it would be kind of dark and dank." In reality, it was light and airy and beautifully decorated. And so enormous! A person could get hopelessly lost wandering the long, carpeted halls. She could hardly believe she would be spending weeks, maybe even months, there. "I expected stone walls and suits of armor in the halls."

The prince chuckled, a deep, throaty sound. "We're a bit more modern than that. You'll find the guest rooms have all the amenities and distinction you would expect from a five-star hotel."

Not that she would know the difference, seeing as how she'd never been in anything more luxurious than a Days Inn.

"Although…" He paused and looked over at her. "The only feasible place for the lab, short of building a new facility on the grounds, was the basement."

She shrugged. It wouldn't be the first time she'd worked in a basement lab. "That's fine with me."

"It used to be a dungeon."

Her interest piqued. "Seriously?"

He nodded. "Very dark and dank at one time, complete with chains on the wall and torture devices."

She gazed at him skeptically. "You're joking, right?"

"Completely serious. It's been updated since then of course. We use it for food and dry storage, and the wine cellar. The laundry facilities are down there, as well. I think you'll be impressed with the lab. Not dark or dank at all."

Because the majority of her time would be spent staring in a microscope or at a computer screen, what the lab looked like didn't matter all that much to her. As long as it was functional.

He led her through an enormous kitchen bustling with activity and rich with the scents of fresh baked bread and scintillating spices. Her stomach rumbled and she tried to recall the last time she'd eaten. She'd been way too nervous to eat the meal offered on the plane.

There would be time for food later.

Aaron stopped in front of a large wood door that she assumed led to the basement. "There's a separate employee entrance that the laundry staff use. It leads outside, to the back of the castle. But as a guest, you'll use the family entrance."

"Okay."

He reached for the handle but didn't open the door. "There is one thing I should probably warn you about."

Warn her? That didn't sound good. "Yes?"

"As I said, the basement has been updated."

"But…?"

"It did used to be a dungeon."

She wasn't getting his point. "Okay."

"A lot of people died down there."

Was she going to trip over bodies on her way to the lab or something? "Recently?"

He laughed. "No, of course not."

Then she wasn't seeing the problem. "So…?"

"That bothers some people. And the staff is convinced it's haunted."

Liv looked at him as though he'd gone completely off his rocker.

"I take it you don't believe in ghosts," Aaron said.

"The existence of spirits, or an afterlife, have never been proven scientifically."

He should have expected as much from a scientist. "Well, then, I guess you have nothing to fear."

"Do you?" she asked.

"Believe in ghosts?" Truthfully, he'd never felt so much as a cold draft down there, but people had sworn to hearing disembodied voices and seeing ghostly emanations. There were some members of the staff who refused to even set foot on the stairs. Also there was an unusually high turnover rate among the laundry workers. But he was convinced that it was more likely overactive imaginations than anything otherworldly. "I guess you could say I try to keep an open mind."

He opened the door and gestured her down. The stairwell was narrow and steep, the wood steps creaky under their feet as they descended.

"It is a little spooky," she admitted.

At the bottom was a series of passageways that led to several different wings. The walls down here were still fashioned out of stone and mortar, although well lit, ventilated and clean.

"Storage and the wine cellar are that way," he said, pointing to the passages on the left. "Laundry is straight ahead down the center passage, and the lab is this way."

He led her to the right, around a corner to a shiny metal door with a thick glass window that to him looked completely out of place with its surroundings. He punched in his security code to unlock it, pulled it open and hit the light switch. The instant the lights flickered on he heard a soft gasp behind him, and turned to see Liv looking in wide-eyed awe at all the equipment they'd gotten on loan from various facilities on the island and mainland. The way one might view priceless art. Or a natural disaster.

She brushed past him into the room. "This is perfect," she said in that soft, breathy voice, running her hands along pieces of equipment whose purpose he couldn't begin to imagine. Slow and tender, as if she were stroking a lover's flesh.

Damn. He could get turned on watching her do that, imagining those hands roaming over him.

If she were his type at all, which she wasn't. Besides, he wasn't lacking for female companionship.

"It's small," he said.

"No, it's perfect." She turned to him and smiled, a dreamy look on her face. "I wish my lab back home were this complete."

He was surprised that it wasn't. "I was under the impression that you were doing some groundbreaking research."

"Yes, but funding is an issue no matter what kind of work you're doing. Especially when you're an independent, like me."

"There must be someone willing to fund your research."

"Many, but there's *way* too much bureaucracy in the private sector. I prefer to do things my way."

"Then our donation should go far."

She nodded eagerly. "The truth is, a few more weeks and I might have been homeless. You called in the nick of time."

She crossed the room to the metal shipping containers that had preceded her arrival by several days. "I see my things made it safely."

"Do you need help unpacking?"

She vigorously shook her head. "There are sensitive materials and equipment in here. I'd rather do it myself."

That seemed like an awful lot of work for one person. "The offer for the assistant is still good. I can have someone here Friday morning."

She looked at her watch, her face scrunching with confusion. "And what's today? The time change from the U.S. has me totally screwed up."

"It's Tuesday. Five o'clock."

"P.M.?"

"Yes. In fact, dinner is at seven."

She nodded, but still looked slightly confused.

"Out of curiosity, when was the last time you slept?"

She scrunched her face again, studied her watch for a second, then shrugged and said, "I'm not sure. Twenty hours at least. Probably more."

"You must be exhausted."

"I'm used to it. I keep long hours in the lab."

Twenty hours was an awfully long time, even for a workaholic, and he'd traveled often enough to know what jet lag could do to a person. Especially someone unaccustomed to long plane trips. "Maybe before you tackle unpacking the lab you should at least take a nap."

"I'm fine, really. Although, I guess I wouldn't mind a quick change of clothes."

"Why don't I show you to your room."

She looked longingly at all of the shiny new equipment, then nodded and said, "All right."

He switched off the lights and shut the door, hearing it lock automatically behind him.

"Will I get my own code?" she asked.

"Of course. You'll have full access to whatever and wherever you need."

He led Liv back through the kitchen and up the stairs to the third floor, to the guest rooms. She looked a bit lost when they finally reached her door.

"The castle is so big and confusing," she said.

"It's not so bad once you learn your way around."

"I don't exactly have a great sense of direction. Don't be surprised if you find me aimlessly wandering the halls."

"I'll have Derek print you up a map." He opened her door and gestured her in.

"It's beautiful," she said in that soft, breathy voice. "So pretty."

Far too feminine and fluffy for his taste, with its flowered walls and frilly drapes, but their female guests seemed to appreciate it. Although he never would have pegged Liv as the girly-girl type. She was just too…analytical. Too practical. On the surface anyhow.

"The bathroom and closet are that way," he said, gesturing to the door across the room. But Liv's attention was on the bed.

"It looks so comfortable." She crossed the room to it and ran one hand over the flowered duvet. "So soft."

She was a tactile sort of woman. Always stroking

and touching things. And he couldn't help but wonder how those hands would feel touching him.

"Why don't you take it for a spin," he said. "The lab can wait."

"Oh, I shouldn't," she protested, but she was already kicking off her shoes and crawling on top of the covers. She settled back against the pillows and sighed blissfully. Her eyes slipped closed. "Oh, this is heavenly."

He hadn't actually meant right that second. The average guest would have waited until he'd left the room, not flop down into bed right in front of him. But he could see that there was nothing average about Olivia Montgomery.

At least she hadn't undressed first. Not that he wasn't curious to see what she was hiding under those clothes. He was beginning to think there was much more to Liv than she let show.

"You'll find your bags in the closet. Are you sure you wouldn't like a maid to unpack for you?"

"I can do it," she said, her voice soft and sleepy.

"If you change your mind, let me know. Other than that, you should have everything you need. There are fresh towels and linens in the bathroom. As well as toiletries. If you need anything else, day or night, just pick up the phone. The kitchen is always open. You're also welcome to use the exercise room or game room, day or night. We want you to feel completely comfortable here."

He walked to the window and pushed the curtain aside, letting in a shaft of late-afternoon sunshine. "You have quite a lovely view of the ocean and the gardens from here. Although there isn't much to see in the gardens this time of year. We could take a walk out there tomorrow."

Or not, he thought, when she didn't answer him. Then he heard a soft rumbling sound from the vicinity of the bed.

She had turned on her side and lay all curled up in a ball, hugging the pillow. He walked over to the bed and realized that she was sound asleep.

"Liv," he called softly, but she didn't budge. Apparently she was more tired than she'd realized.

He found a spare blanket in the closet, noticing her luggage while he was in there, and the conspicuously small amount of it. Just two average-size bags that had seen better days. The typical female guest, especially one there for an extended stay, brought a whole slew of bags.

He reminded himself once again that Liv was not the typical royal guest. And, he was a little surprised to realize, he liked that about her. It might very well be a refreshing change.

He walked back to the bed and covered her with the blanket, then, for reasons he couldn't begin to understand, felt compelled to just look at her for a moment. The angles of her face softened when she slept, making her appear young and vulnerable.

She's not your type, he reminded himself.

If he was going to be honest with himself, his "type" had plenty to offer physically, but intellectually, he was usually left feeling bored and unfulfilled. Maybe it was time for a change of pace.

Seducing a woman like Liv might be just what he needed to spice things up.

Three

It was official. Liv was lost.

She stood in an unfamiliar hallway on what she was pretty sure was the second floor, looking for the staircase that would lead her down to the kitchen. She'd been up and down two separate sets of stairs already this morning, and had wandered through a dozen different hallways. Either there were two identical paintings of the same stodgy-looking old man in a military uniform, or she'd been in this particular hallway more than once.

She looked up one end to the other, hopelessly turned around, wondering which direction she should take. She felt limp with hunger, and the backpack full of books and papers hung like a dead weight off one shoulder. If she didn't eat soon, her blood sugar was going to dip into the critical zone.

She did a very scientific, eenie-meenie-minie-moe, then went left around the corner and plowed face-first into a petite, red-haired maid carrying a pile of clean linens. The force of the collision knocked her off balance and the linens fell to the carpet.

"Oh my gosh! I'm so sorry!" Liv crouched down to pick them up. "I wasn't watching where I was going."

"It's no problem, miss," the maid said in a charming Irish brogue, kneeling down to help. "You must be our scientist from the States. Miss Montgomery?"

Liv piled the last slightly disheveled sheet in her arms and they both stood. "Yes, I am."

The maid looked her up and down. "Well, you don't much look like a scientist."

"Yeah, I hear that a lot." And she was always tempted to ask what she did look like, but she was a little afraid of the answer she might get.

"I'm Elise," the maid said. "If you need anything at all, I'm the one to be asking."

"Could you tell me where to find the kitchen? I'm starving."

"Of course, miss. Follow this hallway down and make a left. The stairs will be on your right, about halfway down the hall. Take them down one flight, then turn right. The kitchen is just down the way."

"A left and two rights. Got it."

Elise smiled. "Enjoy your stay, miss."

She disappeared in the direction Liv had just come from. Liv followed her directions and actually found the kitchen, running into—although not literally this time—Prince Aaron's assistant just outside the door.

"Off to work already?" he asked.

"Looking for food actually. I missed dinner last night."

"Why don't you join the prince in the family dining room."

"Okay." She could spend another twenty minutes or so looking for the dining room, and possibly collapse from hunger, or ask for directions. "Could you show me where it is?"

He smiled and gestured in the opposite direction from the kitchen. "Right this way."

It was just around the corner. A surprisingly small but luxurious space with French doors overlooking the grounds. A thick blanket of leaves in brilliant red, orange and yellow carpeted the expansive lawn and the sky was a striking shade of pink as the sun rose above the horizon.

At one end of a long, rectangular cherry table, leaning casually in a chair with a newspaper propped beside him, sat Prince Aaron. He looked up when they entered the room, then rose to his feet.

"Well, good morning," he said with a smile, and her stomach suddenly bound up into a nervous knot.

"Shall I take your bag?" Derek asked her.

Liv shook her head. That backpack had all of her research. She never trusted it to anyone else. "I've got it, thanks."

"Well, then, enjoy your breakfast," Derek said, leaving her alone with the prince. Just the two of them.

Only then did it occur to her that she might have been better off eating alone. What would they say to each other? What could they possibly have in common? A prince and an orphan?

The prince, on the other hand, looked completely at ease. In jeans and a flannel shirt he was dressed much more casually than the day before. He looked so…*normal*. Almost out of place in the elegant room.

He pulled out the chair beside his own. "Have a seat."

As she sat, she found herself enveloped in the subtle, spicy scent of his aftershave. She tried to recall if William, her possibly-soon-to-be fiancé, wore aftershave or cologne. If he had, she'd never noticed.

The prince's fingers brushed the backs of her shoulders as he eased her chair in and she nearly jolted against the sudden and intense zing of awareness.

He was *touching* her.

Get a grip, Liv. It wasn't like he was coming on to her. He was being *polite* and she was acting like a schoolgirl with a crush. Even when she *was* a schoolgirl she had never acted this way. She'd been above the temptation that had gotten so many other girls from high school in trouble. Or as her last foster mom, Marsha, used to put it, *in the family way.*

Then the prince placed both hands on her shoulders and her breath caught in her lungs.

His hands felt big and solid and warm. You are not going to blush, she told herself, but already she could feel a rush of color searing her cheeks, which only multiplied her embarrassment.

It was nothing more than a friendly gesture, and here she was having a hot flash. Could this be any more humiliating?

"Do you prefer coffee or tea?" he asked.

"Coffee, please," she said, but it came out high and squeaky.

He leaned past her to reach for the carafe on the table, and as he did, the back of her head bumped the wall of his chest. She was sure it was just her imagination, but she swore she felt his body heat, heard the steady thump of his heart beating. Her own heart was hammering so hard that it felt as though it would beat its way out of her chest.

Shouldn't a servant be doing that? she wondered as he poured her a cup and slid it in front of her. Then he *finally* backed away and returned to his chair, resuming the same casual, relaxed stance—and she took her first full breath since she'd sat down.

"Would you care for breakfast?" he asked.

"Please," she said, though her throat was so tight,

she could barely get air to pass through, much less food. But if she didn't eat something soon, she would go into hypoglycemic shock. She just hoped she didn't humiliate herself further. She was so used to eating at her desk in the lab, or in a rush over the kitchen sink, she was a little rusty when it came to the rules of etiquette. What if she used the wrong fork, or chewed with her mouth open?

He rang a bell, and within seconds a man dressed in characteristic butler apparel seemed to materialize from thin air.

"Breakfast for our guest, Geoffrey," he said.

Geoffrey nodded and slipped away as stealthily as he'd emerged.

Liv folded her hands in her lap and, because most of her time was spent huddled over her laptop or a microscope, reminded herself to sit up straight.

"I trust you slept well," the prince said.

She nodded. "I woke at seven thinking it was last night, then I looked outside and noticed that the sun was on the wrong side of the horizon."

"I guess you were more tired than you thought."

"I guess so. But I'm anxious to get down to the lab. You said I'll get a password for the door?"

"Yes, in fact…" He pulled a slip of paper from his shirt pocket and handed it to her. As she took it, she felt lingering traces of heat from his body and her cheeks flushed deeper red.

She unfolded the paper and looked at the code—

a simple seven-digit number—then handed it back to him.

"Don't you want to memorize it?" he asked.

"I just did."

His eyes widened with surprise, and he folded the paper and put it back in his pocket. "Your ID badge will be ready this morning. You'll want to wear it all the time, so you're not stopped by security. It will grant you full access to the castle, with the exception of the royal family's quarters of course, and any of our agricultural facilities or fields."

"You mentioned something about a map of the castle," she said, too embarrassed to admit that she'd actually gotten lost on her way to breakfast.

"Of course. I'll have Derek print one up for you."

"Thank you."

"So," Prince Aaron said, lounging back in his chair and folding his hands in his lap. "Tell me about yourself. About your family."

"Oh, I don't have any family."

Confusion wrinkled his brow. "Everyone has family."

"I'm an orphan. I was raised in the New York foster care system."

His expression sobered. "I'm sorry, I didn't know."

She shrugged. "No reason to be sorry. It's not your fault."

"Do you mind my asking what happened to your parents?"

It's not like her past was some big secret. She had always embraced who she was, and where she came from. "No, I don't mind. My mom died a long time ago. She was a drug addict. Social services took me away from her when I was three."

"What about your father?"

"I don't have one."

At the subtle lift of his brow, she realized how odd that sounded, like she was the product of a virgin birth or something. When the more likely scenario was that her mother had been turning tricks for drug money, and whoever the man was, he probably had no idea he'd fathered a child. And probably wouldn't care if he did know.

She told the prince, "Of course *someone* was my father. He just wasn't listed on my birth certificate."

"No grandparents? Aunts or uncles?"

She shrugged again. "Maybe. Somewhere. No one ever came forward to claim me."

"Have you ever tried to find them?"

"I figure if they didn't want me back then, they wouldn't want me now, either."

He frowned, as though he found the idea disturbing.

"It's really not a big deal," she assured him. "I mean, it's just the way it's always been. I learned to fend for myself."

"But you did have a foster family."

"*Families,*" she corrected. "I had twelve of them."

His eyes widened. "Twelve? Why so many?"

"I was…difficult."

A grin ticked at the corner of his mouth. *"Difficult?"*

"I was very independent." And maybe a little arrogant. None of her foster parents seemed to appreciate a child who was smarter than them and not afraid to say so, and one who had little interest in following their *rules.* "I was emancipated when I was fifteen."

"You were on your own at *fifteen?"*

She nodded. "Right after I graduated from high school."

He frowned and shook his head, as if it was a difficult concept for him to grasp. "Forgive me for asking, but how does an orphan become a botanical geneticist?"

"A *lot* of hard work. I had some awesome teachers who really encouraged me in high school. Then I got college scholarships and grants. And I had a mentor." One she might actually be marrying, but she left that part out. And that was a big *might.* William had never given her this breathless, squishy-kneed feeling when he touched her. She never felt much of anything beyond comfortable companionship.

But wasn't that more important than sexual attraction? Although if she really wanted to marry William, would she be spending so much time talking herself into it?

The butler reappeared with a plate that was all but

overflowing with food. Plump sausages and eggs over easy, waffles topped with cream and fresh fruit and flaky croissants with a dish of fresh jam. The scents had her stomach rumbling and her mouth watering. "It looks delicious. Thank you."

He nodded and left. Not a very talkative fellow.

"Aren't you eating?" she asked Prince Aaron.

"I already ate, but please, go ahead. You must be famished."

Starving. And oddly enough, the prince had managed to put her totally at ease, just as he'd done the night before. He was just so laid-back and casual. So...*nice*. Unlike most men, he didn't seem to be put off or intimidated by her intelligence. And when he asked a question, he wasn't just asking to be polite. He really listened, his eyes never straying from hers while she spoke. She wasn't used to talking about herself, but he seemed genuinely interested in learning more about her. Unlike the scientists and scholars who were usually too wrapped up in their research to show any interest in learning about who she was as a person.

It was a nice change of pace.

The prince's cell phone rang and he unclipped it from his belt to look at the display. Concern flashed across his face. "I'm sorry. I have to take this," he said, rising to his feet. "Please excuse me."

She watched him walk briskly from the room and realized she was actually sorry to see him go. She couldn't recall the last time she'd had a conversation with a man who hadn't revolved in some way around her research, or funding. Not even William engaged in social dialogue very often. It was nice to just talk to someone for a change. Someone who really listened.

Or maybe spending time with the prince was a bad idea. She'd been here less than a day and already she was nursing a pretty serious crush.

Four

"Any news?" Aaron asked when he answered his brother's call.

"We have results back from Father's heart function test," Christian told him.

Aaron's own heart seemed to seize in his chest. Their father, the king, had been hooked to a portable heart pump four months ago after the last of a series of damaging attacks. The procedure was still in the experimental stages and carried risks, but the doctors were hopeful that it would give his heart a chance to heal from years of heart disease damage.

It was their last hope.

Aaron had wanted to accompany his family to

England, but his father had insisted he stay behind to greet Miss Montgomery. *For the good of the country,* he'd said. Knowing he'd been right, Aaron hadn't argued.

Duty first, that was their motto.

"Has there been any improvement?" Aaron asked his brother, not sure if he was ready to hear the answer.

"He's gone from twenty percent heart capacity to thirty-five percent."

"So it's working?"

"Even better than they expected. The doctors are cautiously optimistic."

"That's fantastic!" Aaron felt as though every muscle in his body simultaneously sighed with relief. As a child he had been labeled the easygoing one. Nothing ever bothered Aaron, his parents liked to brag. He was like Teflon. Trouble hit the surface, then slid off without sticking. But he wasn't nearly as impervious to stress as everyone liked to believe. He internalized everything, let it eat away at him. Especially lately, with not only their father's health, but also the diseased crops, and the mysterious, threatening e-mails that had been sporadically showing up in his and his siblings' in-boxes from a fellow who referred to himself, of all things, as the Gingerbread Man. He had not only harassed them through e-mail, but also managed to breach security and trespass on the castle grounds, slipping in and out like a ghost despite added security.

There had been times lately when Aaron felt he was days away from a mandatory trip to the rubber room.

But his father's health was now one concern he could safely, if only temporarily, put aside.

"How much longer do they think he'll be on the pump?" he asked his brother.

"At least another four months. Although probably longer. They'll retest him in the spring."

Aaron had been hoping sooner. On the pump he was susceptible to blood clots and strokes and in rare cases, life-threatening infections. "How is he doing?"

"They had to remove the pump to test his heart and there were minor complications when they reinserted it. Something about scar tissue. He's fine now, but he's still in recovery. They want to keep him here an extra few days. Probably middle of next week. Just to be safe."

As much as Aaron wanted to see his father home, the hospital was the best place for him now. "Is Mother staying with him?"

"Of course. She hasn't left his side. Melissa, the girls and I will be returning Friday as planned."

The girls being Louisa and Anne, their twin sisters, and Melissa, Chris's wife of only four months. In fact, it was on their wedding night that the king had the attack that necessitated the immediate intervention of the heart pump. Though it was in no way Chris and Melissa's fault, they still felt responsible for his sudden downturn.

"Now that Father is improving, maybe it's time you and Melissa rescheduled your honeymoon," Aaron told him.

"Not until he's off the pump altogether," Chris insisted, which didn't surprise Aaron. Chris had always been the responsible sibling. Of course, as crown prince, slacking off had never been an option. But while some people may have resented having their entire life dictated for them, Chris embraced his position. If he felt restricted by his duties, he never said so.

Aaron wished he could say the same.

"Did Miss Montgomery arrive safely?" Chris asked.

"She did. Although her flight was delayed by weather."

"What was your first impression of her?"

He almost told his brother that she was very cute. And despite what she'd told him, he couldn't imagine her as ever being difficult. She was so quiet and unassuming. But he didn't think that was the sort of *impression* Chris was asking for. "She seems very capable."

"Her references all checked out? Her background investigation was clean?"

Did he honestly think Aaron would have hired her otherwise? But he bit back the snarky comment on the tip of his tongue. Until their father was well, Chris was in charge, and that position deserved the same respect Aaron would have shown the king.

"Squeaky-clean," Aaron assured his brother. "And after meeting her, I feel confident she'll find a cure."

"Everyone will be relieved to hear that. I think we should—" There was commotion in the background, then Aaron heard his sister-in-law's voice, followed by a short, muted conversation, as though his brother had put a hand over the phone.

"Is everything okay, Chris?"

"Yes, sorry," Chris said, coming back on the line. "I have to go. They're wheeling Father back to his room. I'll call you later."

"Send everyone my love," Aaron told him, then disconnected, wishing he could be there with his family. But someone needed to stay behind and hold the fort.

He hooked his phone on his belt and walked back to the dining room. Liv was still there eating her breakfast. She had wiped out everything but half of a croissant, which she was slathering with jam. He didn't think he'd ever seen a woman polish off such a hearty meal. Especially a woman so slim and fit.

For a minute he just stood there watching her. She had dressed in jeans and a sweater and wore her hair pulled back into a ponytail again. He couldn't help grinning when he recalled the way she seized up as he put his hands on her shoulders, and the deep blush in her cheeks. He knew he wasn't exactly playing fair, and it was wrong to toy with her, but he'd never met a woman who wore her emotions so blatantly on her sleeve. There was little doubt that she was attracted to him.

She looked up, saw him standing there and smiled. A sweet, genuine smile that encompassed her entire face. She wasn't what he would consider beautiful or stunning, but she had a wholesome, natural prettiness about her that he found undeniably appealing.

"Sorry about that," he told her, walking to the table.

"S'okay," she said with a shrug, polishing off the last of her croissant and chasing it down with a swallow of coffee. "I think that was the most delicious breakfast I've ever eaten."

"I'll pass your compliments on to the chef." Instead of sitting down, he rested his arms on the back of his chair. "I'm sorry to say you won't be meeting my parents until next week."

Her smile vanished. "Oh. Is everything all right?"

"My father's doctors want to keep him a few days longer. Just in case."

"It's his heart?" she asked, and at his questioning look, added, "When I was offered the position, I looked up your family on the Internet. A ton of stuff came back about your father's health."

He should have figured as much. The king's health had been big news after he collapsed at Chris's wedding reception. But other than to say he had a heart "problem," no specific information had been disclosed about his condition.

"He has advanced heart disease," Aaron told her.

Concern creased her brow. "If you don't mind my asking, what's the prognosis?"

"Actually, he's in an experimental program and we're hopeful that he'll make a full recovery."

"He's getting a transplant?"

"He has a rare blood type. The odds of finding a donor are astronomical." He explained the portable heart pump and how it would take over all heart function so the tissue would have time to heal. "He's very fortunate. Less than a dozen people worldwide are part of the study."

"Heart disease is genetic. I'll bet you and your siblings are very health-conscious."

"Probably not as much as we should be, but the queen sees to it that we eat a proper diet. You know how mothers are." Only after the words were out did he realize that no, she probably didn't know, because she'd never had a real mother. He felt a slash of guilt for the thoughtless comment. But if it bothered her, she didn't let it show.

She dabbed her lips with her napkin, then set it on the table beside her plate. Glancing at the watch on her slender wrist, she said, "I should get down to the lab. I have a lot of unpacking to do."

He stepped behind her to pull her chair out, and could swear he saw her tense the slightest bit when his fingers brushed her shoulders. She rose to her feet and edged swiftly out of his reach.

He suppressed a smile. "You're sure you don't need help unpacking?"

She shook her head. "No, thank you."

"Well, then, lunch is at one."

"Oh, I don't eat lunch. I'm usually too busy."

"All right, then, dinner is at seven sharp. You do eat dinner?"

She smiled. "On occasion, yes."

He returned the smile. "Then I'll see you at seven."

She walked to the door, then stopped for a second, looking one way, then the other, as though she wasn't sure which direction to take.

"Left," he reminded her.

She turned to him and smiled. "Thanks."

"I'll remind Derek to get you that map."

"Thank you." She stood there another second, and he thought she might say something else, then she shook her head and disappeared from view.

The woman was a puzzle. Thoughtful and confident one minute, then shy and awkward the next. And he realized, not for the first time, that she was one puzzle he'd like to solve.

After a long morning in the fields and an afternoon in the largest of their greenhouse facilities, Aaron looked forward to a quiet dinner and an evening spent with their guest. Even though normally he would arrange some sort of physical, recreational activity like squash or tennis or even just a walk in the gardens, he was more interested in just talking to Liv. Learning more about her life, her past. She was the first woman in a long time whom he'd found both attractive and intellectually stimulating. And after a few drinks to loosen her up a bit, who knew where the conversation might lead.

He changed from his work clothes and stopped by her room on his way downstairs to escort her to the dining room, but she wasn't there. Expecting her to already be at the table waiting for him, he headed down, but found all of the chairs empty.

Geoffrey stepped in from the pantry.

"Have you seen Miss Montgomery?" Aaron asked.

"As far as I know she's still in the lab, Your Highness."

Aaron looked at his watch. It was already two minutes past seven. Maybe she'd lost track of the time. "Will you wait to serve the first course?"

Geoffrey gave him a stiff nod. "Of course, Your Highness."

A servant of the royal family as long as Aaron could remember, Geoffrey prided himself on keeping them on a strict and efficient schedule. Tardiness was not appreciated or tolerated.

"I'll go get her," Aaron said. He headed through the kitchen, savoring the tantalizing scent of spicy grilled chicken and peppers, and down the stairs to the lab. Through the door window he could see Liv, sitting in front of a laptop computer, typing furiously, papers scattered around her.

He punched in his code and the door swung open,

but as he stepped into the room, Liv didn't so much as glance his way.

Her sweater was draped over the back of her chair and she wore a simple, white, long-sleeved T-shirt with the sleeves pushed up to her elbows. Her ponytail had drooped over the course of the day and hung slightly askew down her back.

"It's past seven," he said softly, so as not to startle her, but got no response. "Liv?" he said, a little louder his time, and still she didn't acknowledge that he was there.

"Olivia," he said, louder this time, and she jolted in her chair, head whipping around. For a second she looked completely lost, as though she had no clue where she was, or who *he* was.

She blinked several times, then awareness slid slowly across her face. "Sorry, did you say something?"

"It's past seven."

She stared at him blankly.

"Dinner," he reminded her.

"Oh…right." She looked down at her watch, then up to her computer screen. "I guess I lost track of time."

"Are you ready?"

She glanced up at him distractedly. "Ready?"

"For *dinner*."

"Oh, right. Sorry."

He gestured to the door. "After you."

"Oh…I think I'll pass."

"Pass?"

"Yeah. I'm right in the middle of something."

"Aren't you hungry?"

She shrugged. "I'll pop into the kitchen later and grab something."

"I can have a plate sent down for you," he said, even though he knew Geoffrey wouldn't be happy about it.

"That would be great, thanks," she said. "By the way, were you down here earlier?"

He shook his head. "I've been in the field all day."

"Does anyone else know the code for the door?"

"No, why?"

"A while ago I looked over and the door was ajar."

"Maybe you didn't close it all the way."

"I'm pretty sure I did."

"I'll have maintenance take a look at it."

"Thanks," she said, her eyes already straying back to the computer screen, fingers poised over the keys.

Geoffrey wouldn't consider it proper etiquette for a guest of the royal family to refuse a dinner invitation and then dine alone at a desk, but even he couldn't argue that Liv was not the typical royal guest.

She could eat in the bathtub for all Aaron cared, as long as she found a cure for the diseased crops.

"I'll have Geoffrey bring something right down."

She nodded vaguely, her attention back on her computer. He opened his mouth to say something else, but realized it would be a waste of breath. Liv was a million miles away, completely engrossed in whatever she was doing.

Doing her job, he reminded himself. They hadn't flown her in and paid good money so that she could spend her time amusing him.

He wondered if this was a foreshadow of what her time here would amount to. And if it was, it was going to be a challenge to seduce a woman who was never around.

Five

Liv studied the data that had been compiled so far regarding the diseased crops and compared the characteristics with other documented cases from all over the world. There were similarities, but no definitive matches yet. She wouldn't know for sure until she compared live samples from other parts of the world, which she would have to order and have shipped with expedited delivery.

She yawned and stretched, thinking maybe it was time for a short break, and heard the door click open.

She dropped her arms and turned to see Prince Aaron walking toward her. At least this time there was actually someone there. Despite a thorough check from a maintenance man, she'd found the door open several times, and once she could swear she'd seen someone peering at her through the window.

"Dinner not to your liking?" he asked.

Dinner? She vaguely remembered Geoffery coming by a while ago.

She followed the direction of his gaze to the table beside her desk and realized a plate had been left for her. Come to think of it, she was a little hungry. "Oh, I'm sure it's delicious. I was just wrapped up in what I was working on."

"I guess you were. You haven't slept, have you?"

"Slept?" She looked at her watch. "It's only ten."

"Ten *a.m.*," he said. "You've been down here all night."

"Have I?" It wouldn't be the first time she'd been so engrossed in her work that she forgot to sleep. Being in a lab with no windows probably didn't help. Unless she looked at her computer clock, which she rarely did, it was difficult to keep track of the time, to know if it was day or night. She'd been known to work for days on end, taking catnaps on her desk, and emerge from the lab with no idea what day it was, or the last time she'd eaten.

And now that she'd stopped working long enough to think about it, she realized that her neck ached and her eyes burned with exhaustion. A good sign that it was time for a break.

"When we hired you, we didn't expect you to

work 24/7," he said, but the playful smile said he was just teasing her.

"It's just the way I work." She reached back to knead the ache that was now spreading from her neck into the slope of her shoulders.

"Neck ache?" he asked, and she nodded. "I'm not surprised. Although gripping the muscles like that is only going to make it hurt more."

"It's stiff," she said.

He expelled an exasperated sigh and shook his head. "Why don't you let me do that."

Him?

She didn't think he was serious...until he stepped behind her chair. He was actually going to do it. He was going to rub her neck. He pushed her hands out of the way, then draped her ponytail over her left shoulder.

"Really," she said. "You don't have to—"

The words died in her throat as his hands settled on her shoulders.

The warmth of his skin began to seep through the cotton of her shirt and her cheeks exploded with heat. And as if that wasn't mortifyingly embarrassing and awkward enough, he slipped his fingers underneath the collar of her shirt. She sucked in a surprised breath as his hands touched her bare skin.

"The trick to relax the muscle," he told her, "is not to pinch the tension out, but to instead apply even pressure."

Yeah, right. Like there was any way she was going

to be able to relax now, with his hands touching her. His skin against her skin.

He pressed his thumbs into the muscle at the base of her neck and, against her will, a sigh of pleasure slipped from her lips. He slid his thumbs slowly upward, applying steady pressure. When he reached the base of her skull, he repeated the motion, until she felt the muscles going limp and soft.

"Feel good?" he asked.

"Mmm." Good didn't even begin to describe the way he was making her feel. Her head lolled forward and her eyes drifted shut.

"It would be better with oil," he said. "Unfortunately I don't have any handy."

The sudden image of Prince Aaron rubbing massage oil onto her naked body flashed through her brain.

Oh, no. Don't even go there, Liv. This was not a sexual come-on. He was just being polite. Although at that moment she would give anything to know what it would feel like. His oily hands sliding across her bare skin…

As if that would ever happen.

He sank his thumbs into the crevice beside her shoulder blades and a gust of breath hissed through her teeth.

"You have a knot here," he said, gently working it loose with his thumbs.

"You're really good at this," she said. "Did you take a class or something?"

"Human anatomy."

"Why would a prince in an agriculturally based field need a human anatomy class?"

"It might surprise you to learn that there was a time when I was seriously considering medical school."

Actually that didn't surprise her at all. She had the feeling there was a lot more to Prince Aaron than he let people see. "What changed your mind?" she asked.

"My family changed it for me. They needed me in the family business, so I majored in agriculture instead. End of story."

Somehow she doubted it was that simple. There was a tense quality to his voice that belied his true feelings.

"I guess that's the benefit of not having parents," she said. "No one to tell you what to do."

"I guess" was all he said, and she had the distinct impression she'd broached a subject he preferred not to explore. He gave her shoulders one last squeeze, then backed away and asked, "Feel better?"

"Much," she said, turning toward him. "Thank you."

"Sure," he said, but the usual, cheery smile was absent from his face. In fact, he looked almost…sad. Then she realized the inference in what she'd just said. His father was *dying,* his only hope a risky experimental procedure, and here she was suggesting that not having parents was a good thing.

Here he was being nice to her, and she was probably making him feel terrible.

Way to go, Liv. Open mouth, insert foot.

"Aaron, what I said just then, about not having parents—"

"Forget it," he said with a shrug.

In other words, *drop it.*

The lack of sleep, especially after that relaxing massage, was obviously taking its toll on her. She was saying stupid and inappropriate things to a man she knew practically nothing about. A virtual stranger.

A stranger who had the authority to fire her on a whim if it suited him.

"You should get some rest," he said.

He was right. She was long overdue for a power nap. "Now, if I can just find my way back to my room," she joked.

"Didn't Derek bring you a map?"

She looked down at her desk, papers strewn everywhere. "It's here. Somewhere."

He smiled and gestured to the door. "Come on, I'll walk you up."

"Thank you." She slipped her laptop in her backpack and slung it over her shoulder, grabbing the plate of uneaten food on her way out.

Even though he was silent, the tension between them seemed to ease as she followed the prince out of the lab and up the stairs. She left the plate in the kitchen and received a distinct look of disapproval from the butler.

"Sorry," she said lamely, and he answered with a stiff nod. That on top of what she'd said to the prince filled her with a nagging sense of guilt as they walked up to her room. She was obviously way out of her league here. This was going to take a lot of getting used to.

When they reached her door, she turned to him and said, "Thanks for walking me up."

He smiled. "My pleasure. Get some rest."

He started to turn away.

"Aaron, wait!"

He stopped and turned back to her.

"Before you go, I wanted to apologize."

His brow furrowed. "For what?"

"What I said in the lab."

"It's okay."

"No, it isn't. It was really...thoughtless. And I'm sorry if I made you feel bad."

"Liv, don't worry about it."

"I mean, I basically suggested you would be better off without parents, which, considering your father's health, was totally insensitive of me. My verbal filter must be on the fritz."

He leaned casually against the doorjamb, a look of amused curiosity on his face. "Verbal filter?"

"Yeah. People's thoughts go through, and the really dumb and inappropriate stuff gets tossed out before they can become words. Lack of sleep must have mine working at minimum capacity. I know it's a pretty lame excuse. But I'm really, *really* sorry. I'm just an employee. I have no right asking you personal questions or talking about your family, anyway."

For several long, excruciating seconds he just looked at her, and she began to worry that maybe he really was thinking about firing her. Then he asked, "Will you have dinner with me tonight?"

Huh?

She insulted him, and he invited her to share dinner with him? She might have thought he was extending a formal invitation just to be polite, but he looked sincere. Like he really *wanted* to have dinner with her.

"Um, sure," she said, more than a touch puzzled.

"Seven sharp."

"Okay."

"I'll warn you that Geoffrey loathes tardiness."

"I'll be on time," she assured him.

He flashed her one last smile, then walked away.

She stepped into her room and shut the door, still not exactly sure what just happened, but way too tired to try to sort it out. She would think about it later, after she'd had some sleep.

As inviting as the bed looked, the draw of a steaming shower was too appealing to resist. The sensation of the hot water jetting against her skin was almost as enjoyable as Aaron's neck massage had been. After her shower she curled up under the covers, planning to sleep an hour or two before heading back down to the lab.

She let her tired, burning eyes drift shut, and when she opened them again to check the clock on the bedside table, it was six forty-five.

* * *

Liv had been so wracked with guilt when Aaron walked her to her room this morning, she hadn't been paying attention to how they got there. And of course her handy map was in the lab, buried under her research. Which was why, four minutes before she was supposed to be in the dinning room, she was frantically wandering the halls, looking for a familiar landmark. The castle was just so big and quiet. If only she would run into someone who could help. She was going to be late, and she had the feeling she was already in hot water with Geoffrey the butler.

She rounded a corner and ran—literally—into someone.

Plowed into was more like it. But this time it wasn't a petite maid. This time it was a hulk of man, built like a tank, who stood at least a foot taller than her own five-foot-ten-inch frame. If he hadn't caught her by the arms, the force of the collision probably would have knocked her on her butt.

He righted and swiftly released her.

"Sorry," she apologized, wondering how many more royal employees she would collide with while she was here. "It was my fault. I wasn't looking where I was going."

"Miss Montgomery, I presume?" he said in a slightly annoyed tone, looking, of all places, at her chest. Then she looked down and realized she'd forgotten to pin on her ID badge. She pulled it from the outer pocket of her backpack and handed it to him. "Yeah, sorry."

His badge identified him as Flynn, and she couldn't help thinking that he looked more like a *Bruno* or a *Bruiser.*

He looked at the photo on her badge, then back at her, one brow raised slightly higher than the other. He didn't say, *You don't look like a scientist,* but she could tell he was thinking it.

He handed it back to her. "You should wear this at all times."

"I know. I forgot." She hooked it on her sweater, managing not to skewer her skin as she had yesterday. "Maybe you can help me. I'm trying to get to the dining room," she told him. "I've lost my way."

"Would you like me to show you the way?"

She sighed with relief. "That would be wonderful. I'm about three minutes from being late for dinner, and I'm already in the doghouse with Geoffrey."

"We can't have that," he said, gesturing in the direction she'd just come from. "This way, miss."

This time she paid attention as he led her downstairs to the dining room and she was pretty sure that she would be able to find her way back to her room. But she would keep the map with her at all times, just in case.

Prince Aaron was sitting in the dining room waiting for her, nursing a drink, when they walked in.

"I found her, Your Highness," Flynn told him.

"Thank you, Flynn," the prince said.

He nodded and left, and Liv realized it was no accident that she'd encountered him in the hallway.

"How did you know I would get lost?" she asked him.

He grinned. "Call it a hunch."

He rose from his chair and pulled out the adjacent chair for her, and as she sat, his fingers brushed the backs of her shoulders. Was he doing it on purpose? And if so, why did he feel the need to touch her all the time? Did he get some morbid kick out of making her nervous?

The only other time she'd had an experience with a touchy-feely person was back in graduate school. Professor Green had had a serious case of inappropriately wandering hands that, on a scale of one to ten, had an ick factor of fifteen. All of his female students fell victim to his occasional groping.

But unlike her professor, when Aaron touched her, she *liked* the way it felt. The shiver of awareness and swift zing of sexual attraction. She just wished she knew what it meant.

He eased her chair in and sat back down, lounging casually, drink in hand. "Would you like a drink? A glass of wine?"

"No, thank you. I have to stay sharp."

"What for?"

"Work."

He frowned. "You're working tonight?"

"Of course."

"But by the time we finish dinner, it will be after eight o'clock."

She shrugged. "So?"

"So, I have an idea. Why don't you take a night off?"

"Take a night off?"

"Instead of locking yourself in the lab, why don't you spend the evening with me?"

Six

The confused look on Liv's face was as amusing as it was endearing. She was as far from his type as a woman could be, yet Aaron wanted inside her head, wanted to know what made her tick.

Geoffrey appeared with the first course of their dinner, a mouthwatering lobster bisque. He knew this because he'd managed to sneak a taste before the chef had chased him out of the kitchen.

"How about that drink?" he asked Liv.

"Just water, please. Bottled, if you have it."

Geoffrey nodded and left to fetch it.

"You never answered my question," he said.

She fidgeted with her napkin. "I'm here to work, Your Highness."

"Aaron," he reminded her. "And you just worked a twenty-four-hour shift. Everyone needs a break every now and then."

"I had a break. I slept all day."

He could see he was getting nowhere, so he tried a different angle: the guilt card. He frowned and said, "Is the idea of spending time with me really so repulsive?"

Her eyes widened and she vigorously shook her head. "No! Of course not! I didn't mean to imply..." She frowned and bit her lip.

He could see that she was this close to giving in, so he made the decision for her. "It's settled, then. You'll spend the evening with me."

She looked hesitant, but seemed to realize that she had little choice in the matter. "I guess one night off wouldn't kill me."

"Excellent. What do you do for fun?"

She stared blankly.

"You do have fun occasionally, right?"

"When I'm not working I read a lot to catch up on the latest scientific discoveries and theories."

He shot her a skeptical look.

"That's fun."

"I'm talking social interaction. Being with other human beings."

He got a blank look from Liv.

"What about sports?" he asked.

She shrugged. "I'm not exactly athletic."

A person would never know it by her figure. She

looked very fit. He knew women who spent hours in the gym to look like Liv, and would kill to have a figure like that naturally.

"Do you go to movies?" he asked. "Watch television?"

"I don't get to the movies very often, and I don't own a television."

This time his eyes widened. "How can you not own a television?"

"What's the point? I'm never home to watch it."

"Music? Theater?"

She shook her head.

"There must be *something* you like to do besides work and read about work."

She thought about it for a moment, chewing her lip in concentration, then she finally said, "There is *one* thing I've always wanted to try."

"What's that?"

"Billiards."

Her answer surprised him. "Seriously?"

She nodded. "It's actually very scientific."

He grinned. "Well, then, you're in luck. We have a billiards table in the game room, and I happen to be an excellent teacher."

Ten minutes into her first billiards lesson, Liv began to suspect that choosing this particular game had been a bad idea. Right about the time that Aaron handed her a cue and then proceeded to stand behind her, leaning her over the edge of the table, his body pressed to hers, and demonstrating the appropriate way to hold it.

Hard as she tried to concentrate on his instructions, as he took her through several practice shots, she kept getting distracted by the feel of his wide, muscular chest against her back. His big, bulky arms guiding her. His body heat penetrating her clothes and warming her skin. And oh, did he smell good. Whatever aftershave or cologne he'd used that morning had long since faded and his natural, unique scent enveloped her.

It's just chemical, she reminded herself. And wholly one-sided. He wasn't holding her like this for pleasure, or as some sort of come-on. He was giving her a billiards lesson. Granted, she'd never had one before, but it stood to reason this was the way one would do it. Although the feel of him guiding the cue, sliding it back and forth between her thumb and forefinger, was ridiculously erotic.

If he did have some other sort of lesson on his mind, one that had nothing to do with billiards, she was so far out of her league that she couldn't even see her own league from here. Although, she had to admit, the view here was awfully nice.

"Have you got that?" Aaron asked.

She realized all this time he'd been explaining the game to her and she had completely zoned out. Which was absolutely unlike her. She turned her head toward him and he was so close her cheek collided with his chin. She could feel his breath shifting the wisps of hair that had escaped her ponytail.

She jerked her head back to look at the table, swallowing back a nervous giggle. Then she did something that she hardly ever did, at least, not since she was a rebellious teen. She *lied* and said, "I think I've got it."

He stepped back, racked up the balls, then said, "Okay, give it a try."

She lined the cue up to the white ball, just the way he'd shown her, but she was so nervous that when she took the shot she hit the green instead, leaving a chalky line on the surface. She cringed and said, "Sorry."

"It's okay," he assured her. "Try it again, but this time get a little closer to the ball. Like this." He demonstrated the motion with his own cue, then backed away.

She leaned back over, following his actions, and this time she managed to hit the ball, but the force only moved it about six inches to the left, completely missing the other balls, before it rolled to a stop. "Ugh."

"No, that was good," he assured her. "You just need to work on your aim and put a little weight behind it. Don't be afraid to give it a good whack."

"I'll try."

He set the cue ball back in place and she leaned over, lining it up, and this time she really whacked it. A little too hard, because the ball went airborne, banking to the left, right off the table. She cringed as it landed with a sharp crack on the tile floor. "Sorry!"

"It's okay," he said with a good-natured chuckle, rounding the table to fetch the ball. "Maybe not quite so hard next time."

She frowned. "I'm terrible at this."

"You just started. It takes practice."

That was part of the problem. She didn't have *time* to practice. Which was exactly why she was hesitant to try new things. Her motto had always been, If you can't be the best at something, why bother?

"Watch me," he said.

She stepped aside to give him room. He bent over and lined up the shot, but instead of keeping her eyes on his cue, where they were supposed to be, she found herself drawn to the perfect curve of his backside. His slacks hugged him just right.

She heard a loud crack, and lifted her gaze to see the balls scattering all over the table.

"Just like that," he said, and she nodded, despite the fact that, like before, she hadn't been paying attention. He backed up and gestured to the table. "Why don't you knock a few around. Work on your aim."

Despite her awkwardness, somehow Aaron always managed to make her feel less…inept. And after some practice and a couple of false starts, she was actually getting the hang of it. She even managed to keep all the balls on the table where they belonged and sink a few in the pockets. When they played a few actual games, she didn't do too badly, although she had the sneaking suspicion he was deliberately going easy on her.

After a while, despite having slept most of the day, she started yawning.

"Maybe we should call it a night," he said.

"What time is it?"

"Half past twelve."

"Already!" She had no idea they'd been playing that long.

"Past your bedtime?" he teased.

"Hardly." As if on cue, she yawned again, so deeply moisture filled her eyes. "I don't know why I'm so sleepy."

"Probably jet lag. It'll just take a few days for your system to adjust. Why don't you go to bed and get a good night's sleep, then start fresh in the morning."

As eager as she was to get back down to the lab, he was probably right. Besides, she really needed samples and her assistant wouldn't be here until the next morning. Maybe she could take some time to catch up on a bit of reading.

"I think maybe I will," she told him.

He took her cue and hung it, and his own, on a wall rack. "Maybe we can try this again, tomorrow night."

"Maybe," she said, and the weird thing was that she really wanted to. She was having fun. Maybe *too* much fun. She had a job to do here. That disease wasn't going to cure itself. It had been hours since she'd even thought about her research, and that wasn't at all like her.

"I'll walk you to your room," Aaron said.

"I think I can find my way." They were some-where on the third floor, and if she took the nearest steps down one floor she was pretty sure she would be near the hallway her room was on.

"A gentleman always walks his date to the door," he said with a grin. "And if nothing else, I am *always* a gentleman."

Date? Surely he was using that word in the loosest of terms, because she and Aaron were definitely not *dating*. Not in the literal sense. He meant it casually, like when people said they had a *lunch date* with a friend. Or a *dinner date* with a work associate.

She picked up her backpack from where she'd left it by the door, slung it over her shoulder and followed him out into the hall and down the stairs. She wanted to remember how to get there, should she ever decide to come back and practice alone every now and then.

"By the way, do you play poker?" he asked as they walked side by side down the hall toward her room.

"Not in a long time."

"My brother, sister and I play every Friday night. You should join us."

"I don't know…"

"Come on, it'll be fun. I promise, it's much easier than billiards."

She wondered if that would be considered proper. The hired help playing cards with the family. Of course, since she'd arrived, he'd treated her more like a guest than an employee.

"If you claim you have to work," he said sternly, "I'll change the door code and lock you out of the lab."

She couldn't tell if he was just teasing her, or if he would really do it. And who knows, it might be fun. "They won't mind?"

"My brother and sister? Of course not. We always invite palace guests to join in."

"But I'm not technically a guest," she said as they stopped in front of her door. "I work for you."

He was silent for a moment as he seemed to digest her words, looking puzzled. Finally he said, "You don't have the slightest clue how valuable you are, do you?"

His words stunned her. Her? Valuable?

"What you've been through. What you've *overcome*..." He shook his head. "It makes me feel very insignificant."

"I make you feel that way?" she asked, flattening a hand to her chest. *"Me?"*

"Why is that so hard to believe?"

"You're royalty. Compared to you, I'm nobody."

"Why would you think you're nobody?"

"Because...I am. What have I ever done?"

"You've done a hell of a lot more than I ever have. And think of all that you still have the chance to do."

She could hardly believe that Aaron, a *prince,* could possibly hold someone like her in such high esteem. What was he seeing that no one else did?

"I'm sure you've done things, too," she said.

He shook his head. "All of my life I've had things

handed to me. I've never had to work for *anything*. And look at the adversity you've overcome to get where you are."

She shrugged. "I just did what I had to do."

"And that's my point exactly. Most people would have given up. Your determination, your *ambition*, is astounding. And the thing I like most is that you don't put on airs. You don't try to be something that you're not." He took a step closer and his expression was so earnest, so honest, her breath caught. "I've never met a woman so confident. So comfortable in her own skin."

Confident? Was he serious? She was constantly second-guessing herself, questioning her own significance. Her worth.

"You're intelligent and interesting and kind," he said. "And fun. And I'm betting that you don't have a clue how beautiful you are."

Did the guy need glasses? She was so…plain. So unremarkable. "You think I'm beautiful?"

"I don't think you are. I *know* you are. And you wouldn't believe how much I've wanted to…" He sighed and shook his head. "Never mind."

She was dying to know what he was thinking, and at the same time scared to death of what it might be. But her insatiable curiosity got the best of her.

Before she could stop herself she asked, "You wanted to do what?"

For a long, excruciating moment he just looked at

her and her heart hammered relentlessly in anticipation. Finally he grinned that sexy simmering smile and told her, "I wanted do this." Then he wrapped a hand around the back of her neck, pulled her to him and kissed her.

This was not the wishy-washy version of a kiss that Liv had gotten from William the day she left. Not even close. This kiss had heart. And soul. It had soft lips and caressing hands and breathless whimpers—mostly from her.

It was the kind of kiss that a girl remembered her entire life, the one she looked back on as her first *real* kiss. And she was kissing him back just as enthusiastically. Her arms went around Aaron's neck, fingers tunneled through his hair. She was practically *attacking* him, but he didn't seem to mind. She felt as though she needed this, needed to feed off his energy, like a plant absorbing the sunlight.

She kept waiting for him to break the kiss, to laugh at her and say, *Just kidding* or *I can't believe you fell for that!* As if it was some sort of joke. What other reason would he have for kissing someone like her? But he didn't pull away. He pulled *her* closer. Her breasts crushed against the solid wall of his chest, tingling almost painfully, and just like that, she was hotter and more turned on than she'd ever been in her life.

But what about William?
William who?

Aaron's hands were caressing her face, tangling through her hair, pulling the band free so it spilled out around her shoulders. He pulled her closer and she nearly gasped when she felt the length of his erection, long and stiff against her belly. Suddenly the reality of what she was doing, where this was leading and the eventual conclusion, penetrated the lusty haze that was clouding her otherwise-rational brain. In the back of her mind a guilty little voice asked, *Is this how you treat the man who asked you to marry him?*

She didn't want to think about that. She wanted to shut him out of her mind, pretend William didn't exist. But he *did* exist, and he was back in the States patiently awaiting an answer from her. Trusting that she was giving his proposal serious thought.

She broke the kiss and burrowed her head against Aaron's shoulder, feeling the deep rise and fall of his chest as he breathed, the rapid beat of his heart. Her own breath was coming in shallow bursts and her heart rate had climbed to what must have been a dangerously high level. Had anyone under the age of seventy ever actually died of heart failure brought on by extreme sexual arousal?

"What's wrong?" he asked, genuine concern in his voice.

She struggled to catch her breath, to slow her pounding heart. "We're moving too fast."

He chuckled. "Um, technically, we haven't actually done anything yet."

"And we shouldn't. We *can't.*"

He was quiet for several seconds, then he asked, "Are you saying you don't want to? Because, love, that kiss was hot as hell."

He called her *love.* No one had ever used a term of endearment like that with her. Certainly not her foster parents. Not even William. It made her feel special. Which made what she had to do next that much harder.

"I want to," she said. "A lot."

He rubbed his hands softly up and down her back. "Are you...afraid?"

She shook her head against his shoulder. She was anything but frightened, although maybe she should have been, because nothing about this made any sense. It wasn't logical, and her entire life revolved around logic and science.

Maybe that was what made it so appealing.

"There's something I haven't told you," she said.

"What is it?"

She swallowed the lump in her throat and looked up at him. "I'm kind of...engaged."

Seven

"You're *engaged?*" Aaron backed away from Liv, wondering why this was the first time he'd heard this. Especially when he considered all of the blatant flirting that had been going both ways between them the past couple of days. Well, some of it went both ways, but in all fairness he was always the one to initiate it.

"Um…sort of," she said, looking uneasy.

Sort of? "Wait, how can a person be *sort of* engaged? And if you are engaged, why aren't you wearing a ring?"

"We kinda didn't get to that part yet."

He narrowed his eyes at her. "What part did you get to exactly?"

"He asked me, and I told him I would think about it."

There was this feeling, low in his gut. A surge of sensation that he didn't recognize. The he realized he was jealous. He envied a complete stranger. "Who is *he?*"

"His name is William. We work together."

"Another scientist?"

She nodded. "He's my mentor."

"Are you in love with him?" he asked.

She hesitated a moment, then said, "He's a good friend. I have an immense amount of respect for him."

Was that relief he'd just felt? "That isn't what I asked you."

She chewed her lip, as though she was giving it deep consideration, then she said, "Love is highly overrated."

Normally he would have agreed, but this was different. *She* was different. He couldn't imagine Liv being happy with a man she only *respected*. She deserved better. She'd fought all of her life to get exactly what she wanted. Why quit now?

And how did he know *what* she wanted when he barely knew her?

Somehow, he just did. And she was special. He couldn't even vocalize exactly why. It was just something he knew deep down.

"He must be a damned good shag, then," Aaron said, aware of how peevish he sounded.

He expected a snappy response, a firm, *Butt out, buster,* or *Mind your own business.* Instead Liv bit her lip and lowered her eyes. It didn't take him long to figure out what that meant.

He folded his arms across his chest and said, "You haven't slept with him, have you?"

"I didn't say that."

But she didn't deny it, either. "Out of curiosity, how long have you been dating this William fellow?"

Her gaze dropped to her feet again and in went the lip between her teeth. She didn't say a word. But her silence said it all.

"Are you telling me that you two have never even dated? Let me guess, you've never kissed him, either?"

She leveled her eyes on him. "I have so!"

He took a step toward her. "I'll bet he doesn't make you half as hot as I do."

He could tell by her expression, from the sudden rush of color to her cheeks, that he was right.

"I wasn't *that* hot," she said, but he knew it was a lie.

"You won't be happy," he said. "You're too passionate."

She looked at him like he was nuts. "I've been accused of a lot of things, but being passionate is not one of them."

He sighed. "There you go, selling yourself short again."

She shook her head in frustration. "I can't believe we're having this conversation. I hardly even know you."

"I know. And that's the bizarre part, because for some reason I feel as though I've known you forever." He could see by her expression that she didn't know how to respond to that, and she wasn't sure what to make of him. And oddly enough, neither did he. This wasn't at all like him.

She grabbed the knob and opened her door. "I should get to sleep."

He nodded. "Promise me you'll think about what I said."

"Good night, Aaron." She slipped inside her room and closed the door behind her.

He turned and walked in the direction of his own room. What he'd told her wasn't a lie. He'd never met anyone quite like her. She sincerely had no idea how unique, how gifted she was.

At first he'd planned only to seduce Liv and show her a good time while she was here, but something had happened since then. Something he hadn't expected. He really *liked* her. And the idea of her marrying this William person—a man she obviously didn't love— disturbed him far more than it should have.

Liv closed the door and leaned against it, expelling a long, deep breath.

What the heck had just happened out there? What did he want from her? Was he just trying to seduce her? To soften her up with his sweet words? Or did he really mean what he said? Did he really think she was interesting and fun? And *beautiful.* And if she really was, why had no one told her until now?

Just because no man had said the words, it didn't mean it wasn't true. And although she would never admit it to his face, he was right about one thing, no man had ever made her even close to as hot as he just had. With barely more than a kiss. Had it gone any further, she may have become the first scientifically genuine victim of spontaneous human combustion.

And oh how she had wanted it to go further. But to what end? A brief, torrid affair? Yeah, so what if it was? What was so wrong with that? They were consenting adults.

Yeah, but what about William?

So what if William wasn't an above-average kisser, and who cared that he didn't get her all hot and bothered the way Aaron did. William was stable and secure, and he respected her, and she was sure that he thought she was beautiful, too. He just wasn't the type of man to express his feelings. She was sure that once they were married he would open up.

But what if he didn't? Was that enough for her?

She heard a muffled jingle coming from her backpack and realized her phone was ringing. She pulled it out and saw that it was, *speak of the devil,* William. She hadn't spoken to him since she left the States. No doubt he was anxious for an answer.

She let it go to voice mail. She would call him

back tomorrow once she'd had a night to think things through. When she'd had time to forget how Aaron's lips felt against hers, and the taste of his mouth, and what it had been like to have his arms around her, his fingers tangling in her hair.

What if she never forgot? Could she go through life always wondering *what if?* Would it really be so awful, for once in her life, to do something just because she wanted to. Because it felt good. It wasn't as if he would want a relationship, and frankly, neither would she. Just one quick roll in the hay. Or maybe two. Then she could go home to William, who would never be the wiser…and live the rest of her life in guilt for betraying him.

Ugh.

But if they weren't technically engaged yet, could it really be counted as cheating?

As she was changing into her pajamas, her cell phone rang again. It was William. She considered letting it go to voice mail again, then decided she at least owed him a few words.

When she answered, his voice was filled with relief.

"I thought maybe you were avoiding me." He sounded so apprehensive and vulnerable. So unlike the confident, steadfast man she was used to, and the truth was, hearing him that way was just the slightest bit…off-putting. It knocked the pedestal she'd always kept him up on down a notch or two.

"Of course not," she said. "I've just been very busy."

"Is this a bad time? I could call back later."

"No, this is fine. I was just getting ready for bed. How have you been?"

"Swamped." He gave her a rundown on everything that had been going on in the lab since she left.

When he'd finished his dissertation, she asked him again. "How are *you*, William?"

"Me?" He sounded confused, probably because they never really talked about their personal lives.

"Yes, *you*."

Finally he said, "Good. I'm good."

She waited for him to elaborate, but he didn't. Instead he asked, "How are *you?*"

Exhausted, but excited, and having more fun than I've ever had in my life, not to mention nursing a pretty serious crush, and considering an affair with, of all people, a prince.

But she couldn't tell him that. "I'm…good."

"The reason for my call," he said, getting right to the point—because William *always* had a point. "I was just wondering if you'd given any thought to my proposal."

He said it so drily, as though he were referring to a work proposal and not a lifetime commitment.

"I have," she said. "It's just…well, I've been so busy. I'd like a little more time to think it over. It's a huge decision."

"Of course. I don't mean to rush you. I realize that it probably came as something of a surprise."

"A little, yes. I never realized you had those kinds of feelings for me."

"You know that I deeply respect you. Both personally and professionally. We make a good team."

Yes, but a good professional relationship and a good marriage were two entirely different animals. Again she had to wonder, did she want to marry a man who respected her, or one who loved her? A man whom she worked well with, or one who found her so sexually appealing he couldn't keep his eyes, or hands, off her? One who made her feel all warm and breathless and squishy inside, the way Aaron did.

Don't even go there, she warned herself. Aaron had no place in this particular equation. Besides, for all she knew William would be fantastic in bed. She'd always considered good sex more of a perk than a necessity.

If that was true, why wasn't she jumping at his offer?

"Can I ask you a question, William?"

"Of course."

"Why now? What's changed from, say, two months ago?"

"Well, I've been doing a lot of thinking lately. I've always imagined that one day I would get married and have a family. And as you know, I'm not getting any younger. It seemed like a good time."

It sounded so logical, but that hadn't exactly been what she was hoping for.

"I guess what I want to know is, why me?"

"Why you?" he said, sounding puzzled. "Why not you?"

"What I mean is, was there a particular reason you asked *me?*"

"Who else would I ask?"

She was seriously fishing here, and he just didn't seem to get it. She wasn't desperate enough to beg for a kind word or two. Like, *You're beautiful* or *I love you.* That would come with time.

Then why, deep down, was a little voice telling her that this was all wrong?

"Things are just so crazy right now," she told him. "Can you give me a few weeks to think about it?"

"Of course," he said, his tone so patient and reasonable that it filled her with shame. "Take your time."

They made random and slightly awkward small talk for several minutes, and William seemed almost relieved when she said she had to go.

She hung up wondering what kind of marriage would they have if the only thing they ever talked about was work? And even worse, he didn't seem all that interested in getting to know her on a personal level. Would that just take time? Or should the years she had already known him have been time enough?

She thought of Aaron, who asked her questions and seemed genuinely interested in getting to know her. Why couldn't William be more like that?

Thoughts like that wouldn't get her anywhere.

William would never be like Aaron—a rich, charming prince. Which was a good thing, because as she'd reminded herself so many times now, Aaron, and men like him, were out of her league. Granted, she had never actually had a relationship with a man like Aaron, but she wasn't so naive that she didn't know the way these things worked. Even if Aaron did find her interesting at first, see her as a novelty, it wouldn't take him long to grow bored with her, for him to realize that she wasn't as special as he thought. Then he would be back to pursuing a proper mate. A woman with the right family and the proper breeding.

Yet she couldn't help but think of all the fun they could have in the meantime.

Eight

Liv was on her way to breakfast the following morning when she was greeted—more like accosted—by one of Aaron's sisters at the foot of the stairs on the main floor. Was it Friday already?

She was nowhere near as tall as her brother and had a slim, frail-looking build, and while they didn't exactly look alike, there was a strong family resemblance. She was dressed in a pale pink argyle sweater and cream-colored slacks and wore her hair pulled back in a low bun. In the crook of one arm she cradled a quivering ball of fur with bulging eyes. A dog, Liv realized. Probably a shih tzu.

The first impression that popped into Liv's head

was sweet and demure. Until the princess opened her mouth.

She squealed excitedly when she saw Liv and said, "You must be Olivia! I'm Aaron's sister Louisa."

Liv was so stunned by her enthusiasm—weren't princesses supposed to be poised and reserved?—she nearly neglected protocol and offered a hand to shake.

"It's nice to meet you, Your Highness," she said, dipping into a slightly wobbly curtsy instead. She had barely recovered when Louisa grabbed her hand and pumped it enthusiastically.

"Call me Louisa." She scratched the canine behind its silky ears. "And this is Muffin. Say hello, Muffin."

Muffin just stared, his little pink tongue lolling out of his mouth.

"I can't tell you how excited we are to have you here," she said, smiling brightly. "Aaron has told us *wonderful* things about you."

Liv couldn't help but wonder exactly what he'd told them. She would be mortified if he'd said something about their kiss last night. Having had the entire night to think it over, she decided that it would definitely never happen again. At least, not until she'd decided what to do about William. Although, probably not then, either. What she needed to concentrate on was the job she had come here to do.

"Has my brother been a good host?" Louisa asked.

Good didn't even begin to describe the sort of

host he'd been. "He has," Liv assured her. "He's made me feel very welcome."

"I'm so glad. I can't *wait* for you to meet the rest of the family! Everyone is so excited that you're here."

"I'm anxious to meet them, too."

"Well, then, let's go. Everyone should be having breakfast."

Everyone? As in, the *entire* family? Louisa expected her to meet them all at once?

Her heart slammed the wall of her chest. She never had been much good in groups of people. She preferred one-on-one interaction. She opened her mouth to object, but Louisa had already looped an arm through hers and was all but dragging her in the direction of the dining room. Liv felt like a giant beside her. Too tall, awkward and totally unrefined.

This was a nightmare.

"Look who I found!" Louisa announced as they entered the dining room. She probably didn't mean to, but she gave the impression that Liv had been aimlessly wandering the halls when this was the first morning she *hadn't* gotten lost.

She did a quick survey of the room and realized that other than Geoffrey, who was serving breakfast, there were no familiar faces. Where was Aaron?

Aaron's brother and his wife sat at one side of the table, while his other sister sat across from them.

"Everyone, this is Olivia Montgomery," Louisa

gushed. "The scientist who has come to save our country!"

Wow, no pressure there. She stood frozen beside Louisa, unsure of what to say or do. Then she felt it. The gentle and soothing pressure of a warm hand on her back. Aaron was standing there to rescue her.

She turned to him, never so happy in her life to see a familiar, friendly face. He was dressed to work in the field, in jeans and a soft-looking flannel shirt over a mock turtleneck.

He must have sensed how tense she was because he said under his breath, so even Louisa wouldn't hear, "Relax, they won't bite."

Miraculously, his deep, patient tone did just that. Her tension and fear seemed to melt away. Most of it at least. As long as Aaron was there, she was confident the introductions would go well. He would never feed her to the wolves.

His hand still on her back, he led her to the table where his brother sat.

"Liv," Aaron said, "meet my brother, Prince Christian, and his wife, Princess Melissa."

"Your Highnesses," she said, dipping into a near-perfect curtsy.

Prince Christian rose to his feet and reached out to shake her hand. She shifted her backpack to the opposite shoulder and accepted it.

His grip was firm and confident, his smile genuine. "I know I speak for everyone when I say it's an honor and a relief to have you here with us."

She pasted on her face what she hoped was a confident and capable smile. "I'm honored to be here."

"If there's anything you need, anything at all, you need only ask."

How about a valium, she was tempted to say, but had the feeling he might not appreciate her brand of humor. Instead she said, "I will, thank you."

"My parents send their regards and apologies that they weren't here to welcome you. They'll return in several days."

Liv wasn't sure if she was supposed to know the facts surrounding their father's situation, so she only nodded.

"You've already met Princess Louisa," Aaron said. "And this is my other sister, Princess Anne."

Louisa and Anne may have been twins, but they didn't look a thing alike. Anne was darker. In color, and considering her guarded expression, in personality, as well.

"Your Highness," Liv said, curtsying in her direction. She was getting pretty good at this.

"I understand you think you can find a cure for the diseased crops," Anne said, sounding slightly antagonistic, as though she questioned Liv's credentials. Was Anne trying to intimidate her? Put her in her place?

It was one thing to question Liv personally, but as a scientist, they wouldn't find anyone more capable.

She lifted her chin a notch. "I don't *think* I can, Your Highness. I *will* find a cure. As I told Prince Aaron, it's simply a matter of time."

A vague smile pulled at the corners of Anne's mouth. If it had been some sort of test, it appeared Liv had passed.

"Shall we sit?" Aaron said, gesturing to the table.

She turned to him. "Actually, I was planning to get right to work."

He frowned. "You're not hungry?"

Not anymore. The idea of sitting and eating breakfast surrounded by his entire family was only slightly less intimidating than facing a firing squad. "If I could get a carafe of coffee sent down to the lab that would be great."

"Of course." He addressed the butler. "Geoffrey, would you take care of that, please?"

Geoffrey nodded, and although Liv couldn't say for sure, he might have looked a bit peeved.

"It was nice to meet everyone," Liv said.

"You'll join us for dinner?" Princess Melissa asked, although it came across as more of a statement than a question.

Before she could form a valid excuse to decline, Aaron answered for her, "Of course she will."

She wanted to turn to him and say, *I will?,* but she held her tongue. Besides, much as she'd like to, she couldn't avoid them forever.

She would feel so much more comfortable if they

treated her like the hired help rather than a guest and left her to her own devices.

"I'll walk you down to the lab," Aaron said, and though her first instinct was to refuse his offer, she didn't want everyone to think there was a reason she shouldn't be alone with him. Like the fact that she was scared to death he would kiss her again. And even more terrified that if he did, she wouldn't be able to make herself stop him this time.

He led her from the room, and when they were in the hall and out of earshot he said, "I know they can be intimidating, especially Anne, but you can't avoid them forever. They're curious about you."

"I just want to get an early start," she lied, "before my assistant arrives."

He shot her a we-both-know-that's-bull look.

"You don't have to walk me to the lab."

"I know I don't." His slightly mischievous grin said he was going to regardless, and the warmth of it began melting her from the inside out. When he rested a hand on her back to lead her there, her skin tingled under his touch.

If this was the way things would be from now on, she was in *big* trouble.

"I think we need to talk," Aaron told Liv as they walked through the kitchen to the basement door.

"About what?" she asked and he shot her a what-do-you-think look. She frowned and said, "Oh, *that*."

"In the lab," he said, "where we can have some privacy." She nodded and followed him silently through the kitchen and down the stairs. She wasn't wound nearly so tight as she'd been facing his family. She'd been so tense when he stepped into the dining room that he was hesitant to touch her for fear that she might shatter.

She trailed him down the stairs and waited while he punched in the door code. When they were in the lab with the door closed, she turned to him and said, "I've decided that what happened last night can't ever happen again."

So, she thought she would use the direct approach. That shouldn't have surprised him. And he was sure she had what she considered a very logical reason for her decision.

He folded his arms across his chest. "Is that so?"

"I'm serious, Aaron." She did look serious. "I talked to William last night."

An unexpected slam of disappointment and envy pegged him right in the gut.

"You've made your decision, then?" he asked, knowing that if she'd said yes to the engagement, he would do everything in his power to talk her out of it. Not for himself of course, but for her sake.

All right, maybe a *little* for himself.

"I haven't made a decision yet, but I told William that I'm still considering it. And until I accept or refuse his proposal, I don't feel it's right to…*see* anyone else."

He grinned. "See."

"You know what I mean."

"Why?"

His question seemed to confuse her. "Why?"

"You're not engaged. Admittedly you're not even *dating* him. So, logically, *seeing* me or anyone else wouldn't technically be considered infidelity."

She frowned. "You're splitting hairs."

"Not to mention that, if you really *wanted* to marry him, why would you need time to think about it? Wouldn't you have said *yes* as soon as he asked?"

She looked troubled, as though she realized he was right, but didn't want to admit it. "It's…complicated."

"And you think it will be less complicated after you're married? You think he'll miraculously change?"

"That's not what I meant."

"It doesn't work that way, Liv. Problems don't go away with the vows. The way I hear it, they usually get worse."

She expelled a frustrated breath. "Why do you even care? Or is this just your way of trying to get me in bed?"

He grinned. "Love, if I wanted in your knickers, I'd have been there last night."

Her cheeks blushed bright pink.

He took a few steps toward her. "I'm not going to insult your highly superior intelligence and say I don't want to get you into bed. But more than that, I like you, Liv, and I don't want to see you make a mistake."

"Ugh! Would you please stop saying that I'm making a mistake?"

"Are you afraid you're going to start believing me?"

"You think that my sleeping with you *wouldn't* be a mistake?"

He knew now that she'd at least been thinking about it. Probably as much as he had. "No, I don't. In fact, I think it would be beneficial to us both."

"Well, you're not exactly biased, are you?" She collapsed in her chair and dropped her head in her hands. "I want to do the right thing, and you're confusing me."

"How could anything *I* say confuse you? Either you want to marry him, or you don't."

"I don't know if I want to marry *anyone* right now!" she nearly shouted, looking shocked at her own words.

Then why fret over it? "If you're not ready to get married, tell him no."

She looked hopelessly confused and completely adorable. He could see that she wasn't used to not having all the answers. For some reason it made him like her that much more.

She gazed up at him, eyes clouded by confusion. "What if I don't get another chance?"

"To marry William?"

"To marry *anyone!* I do want to get married someday and have a family."

"What's stopping you?"

"What if no one else ever asks?"

That was the most ridiculous thing he'd ever heard. She was an attractive, desirable woman that any man would be lucky to have. If she spent some time outside of her lab and living her life, she might already know that. Men would probably be fighting each other to win her hand.

He knelt down in front of her chair, resting his hands on her knees. "Liv, trust me, someone will ask. Someone you want to marry. Someone you *love*."

She gazed into his eyes, looking so young and vulnerable and confused. What was it about her that made him want take her in his arms and just hold her? Soothe her fears and assure her that everything would be okay. But even if he'd wanted to, she didn't give him the chance. Instead, she leaned forward, wrapped her arms around his neck and kissed him.

Nine

That guilty little voice inside Liv was shouting, *Don't do it, Liv!* But by then it was already too late. Her arms were around Aaron's neck and her lips were on his. She was kissing him again, and he was kissing her back. The feel of his mouth, the taste of him, was already as familiar as it was exciting and new. Maybe because she'd spent most of the night before reliving the first kiss and fantasizing what it would feel like to do it again. Now she knew. And it was even better than she remembered. Better than she could ever have imagined.

Aaron cupped her face in his hands, stroking her cheeks, her throat, threading his fingers through her hair. She hooked her legs around his back, drawing him closer, clinging to him. She might have been embarrassed by her brazen behavior, but she felt too hot and needy with desire to care. She needed to feel him. She just plain *needed* him. Nothing in her life had ever felt this good, this…right. She hadn't even known it was possible to feel this way. And she wanted more—wanted it all. Even though she wasn't completely sure what *it* was yet. Was this just physical, or was there more to it?

Of course not. What did she think, they were going to have some sort of relationship? She didn't want that any more than he did. Her work was too important to her.

That didn't mean they couldn't have a little fun.

She tugged the tail of his flannel from the waist of his jeans, but he grabbed her hands and broke the kiss, saying in a husky voice, "We can't."

Shame burned her cheeks. Of course they couldn't. Hadn't she just told him that very same thing? What the hell had she been thinking? Why, the instant she was near him, did she seem to lose all concept of right and wrong?

She jerked her hands free and rolled the chair backward, away from him. "You're right. I'm sorry. I don't know what I was thinking. This isn't like me at all."

He looked puzzled for a moment, then he grinned and said, "I don't mean *ever.* I just meant that we can't *here*. Any minute now Geoffrey is going to walk through that door with your coffee, not to mention the lab assistant who's due here this morning."

"Oh, right," she said, feeling, of all things, relieved. When what she should have felt was ashamed of herself, and regretful for once again betraying William. Although, as Aaron had pointed out, she and William weren't technically a couple.

You're rationalizing, Liv. When there was absolutely nothing rational about this scenario. This was not the way the world was supposed to work. Brainy, orphaned scientists did not have flings with rich, handsome princes. No matter what the storybooks said.

Nothing that felt this wonderful could possibly be good for her.

"We can't do this again," she told him. "Ever."

Aaron sighed. "We're back to that again?"

"It's wrong."

Aaron rose from his knees and tucked his shirt back in. "It felt pretty good to me."

"I'm serious, Aaron."

"Oh, I know you are."

So why didn't he look as though he was taking her seriously? Why did she get the feeling he was just humoring her?

"I have to get to work," he said. "I'll see you at dinner?"

Was that a statement or a request? She could say no, but she suspected he wouldn't take no for an answer, and that if she tried to skip it, he would come down to the lab and fetch her. At least with his family around he wouldn't try anything physical with her. At least, she hoped he wouldn't. She seriously doubted his family would approve of Aaron messing around with the hired help. Especially one who ranked so abysmally low in the social ladder.

"Seven sharp," she said.

He leaned over and before she could stop him, he gave her a quick kiss—just a soft brush of his lips against hers, but it left her aching for more—then he walked to the door. As he opened it, he turned back to her and said, "Don't forget about the poker game tonight." Then he left, the door closing with a metallic click behind him.

Ugh. She had forgotten all about that. But she already said she would play, so she doubted he would let her back out now.

As much as she didn't want to spend the evening with his family, she dreaded even more spending it alone with him.

She turned to her desk, reaching for the pen she'd left beside her keyboard, but it wasn't there. She searched all over the desk, under every paper and text. She even checked the floor, in case it had somehow rolled off the desk, but it wasn't there. It was as if it had vanished into thin air.

She got a new one from her backpack, and as she was leaning over she heard a noise behind her, from the vicinity of the door. She thought maybe it was Geoffrey with her coffee, or her lab assistant, but when she turned, there was no one there.

And the damn door was open again.

After breakfast Aaron pulled Chris aside and asked, "So, what did you think of Liv?"

"Liv?"

"Miss Montgomery."

Chris raised one brow. "We're on a first-name basis, are we?"

Aaron scowled a him. "I'm being serious."

Chris chuckled. "I'll admit she's not at all what I expected. She doesn't look like a scientist and she's much younger than I imagined. She does seem quite confident, though, if not a bit...*unusual.*"

"Unusual?"

"Not the typical royal guest."

Despite having thought that very same thing, Aaron felt protective of Liv. "What does that matter, so long as she gets the job done?"

Chris grinned. "No need to get testy. I'm just making an observation."

"An observation of someone you know nothing about." Knowing his siblings had the tendency to be more judgmental, Aaron wouldn't tell them about Liv's past. Not that he believed she had anything to be ashamed of—quite the contrary in fact—but the things she'd told him had been in confidence. If they wanted to know more about her, they would have to ask themselves—which he didn't doubt they would.

"If I didn't know better, I might think you fancy her," Chris said. "But we all know that you prefer your women with IQs in the double digits."

Even though he couldn't exactly deny the accusation, Aaron glared at him. "By the way, I invited her to our poker game tonight."

Chris looked intrigued. "Really? She doesn't strike me as the card-playing type."

Aaron wanted to ask, *What type does she strike you as?*, but he was afraid he might not like the answer he got. "Are you saying you don't want her to play?"

Chris shrugged. "It's fine with me. The more the merrier." He looked at his watch. "Is there anything else? I have a conference call in fifteen minutes."

"No, nothing else."

Chris started to turn away, then stopped and said, "I almost forgot to ask, have there been any new developments since I left?"

Aaron didn't have to ask Chris what he meant. It had been in the back of everyone's minds for months now. The person who referred to himself as the Gingerbread Man. "No e-mails, no security breaches. Nothing. It's as if he disappeared into thin air."

Chris looked relieved. "I hope that means it was a harmless prank, and we've heard the last of him."

"Or it could mean that he's building up to something big."

His relief instantly turned to irritation. "Always the optimist."

Aaron grinned. "I like to think that I'm realistic. Whoever he was, he went through an awful lot of trouble breaching our security systems. All I'm saying is that we should keep on our toes."

"I'll keep security on high alert, but at some point we'll have to assume he's given up."

"Call it a hunch," Aaron said, "but I seriously doubt we've seen or heard the last of him."

In her life Liv had never met such an inquisitive group of people. It must run in the family because during dinner she was overwhelmed by endless questions from every side of the table. And like their brother, they seemed genuinely interested in her answers. They asked about her work and education mostly, and they were nothing if not thorough. By the end of the evening she felt picked over and prodded, much like one of the soil samples she'd studied that afternoon. It could have been worse. They could have completely ignored her and made her feel like an outsider.

"See?" Aaron whispered as they walked to the game room to play cards. "That wasn't so bad."

"Not too bad," she admitted.

As they took seats around the table, Geoffrey took

drink orders while Prince Christian—Chris, as he'd asked her to address him—divvied out the chips.

"We start with one hundred each," Aaron told her. "I can front you the money."

She hadn't realized they would play for real money. In college and grad school the stakes had been nickels and dimes, but one hundred euros wasn't exactly out of her budget range. She'd checked the exchange rate before leaving the U.S. and one hundred euros would be equivalent to roughly one hundred thirty-one dollars, give or take.

"I can cover it," she told him.

He regarded her curiously. "You're sure?"

Did he think she was that destitute? "Of course I'm sure."

He shrugged and said, "Okay."

She was rusty the first few hands, but then it all started to come back to her and she won the next few rounds. A bit unfairly, she would admit, even though it wasn't exactly her fault. Besides, she was actually having fun.

Louisa apparently didn't play cards. She sat at the table with her dog, to her siblings' obvious irritation, chatting.

"Where are you from originally?" she asked Liv. She was definitely the friendlier of the twins. A glass-is-half-full kind of girl. And Liv used the term *girl* because Louisa had so sweet a disposition.

"I'm from New York," Liv told her.

"Your family still lives there?" she asked.

"Five card draw, nothing wild," Chris announced, shooting Louisa a look as he shuffled the cards.

"I don't have family," Liv said.

"Everyone has some family," Melissa said with the subtle twang of a Southern accent. Aaron had mentioned that she was born on Morgan Isle, the sister country of Thomas Isle, but had been raised in the U.S. in Louisiana.

"None that I know of," Liv told her. "I was abandoned as a small child and raised in foster homes."

"Abandoned?" Melissa repeated, her lower lip beginning to quiver and tears pooling in her eyes. "That's *so* sad."

"Easy, emotio-girl," Chris said, rubbing his wife's shoulder. When the tears spilled over onto her cheeks, he put down the cards he'd been dealing, reached into his pants pocket and pulled out a handkerchief. Neither he nor anyone else at the table appeared to find her sudden emotional meltdown unusual.

Melissa sniffed and dabbed at her eyes.

"You all right?" he asked, giving her shoulder a reassuring squeeze.

She gave him a wobbly nod and a halfhearted smile.

"You'll have to excuse my wife," Chris told Liv. "She's a little emotional these days."

"Just a little," Melissa said with a wry smile. "It's these damn fertility drugs. I feel like I'm on an emotional roller coaster."

"They're trying to get pregnant," Aaron told Liv.

"She's a scientist, genius," Anne said. "I'm sure she knows what fertility drugs are for."

Aaron ignored her.

"I don't know much about it myself, although I have a colleague who specializes in fertility on a genetic level," Liv said. "I never realized how common it is for couples to have some fertility issues."

"We're trying in vitro," Melissa said, tucking the handkerchief in her lap while Chris finished dealing. "Our doctor wanted us to wait and try it naturally for six months, but I'm already in my midthirties and we want at least three children, so we opted for the intervention now."

"We do run the risk of multiples," Chris said. "Even more so because obviously twins run in the family. But it's a chance we're willing to take."

It surprised Liv that they spoke so openly to a stranger about their personal medical issues, although she had found that, because she was a scientist, people assumed she possessed medical knowledge, which couldn't be further from the truth. Unless the patient happened to be a plant.

"I'll open for ten," Aaron said, tossing a chip in the pot, and everyone but Anne followed suit.

She threw down her cards and said, "I fold."

"I can hardly wait to have a little niece or nephew to spoil. Or both!" Louisa gushed. "Do you want children, Olivia?"

"Someday," Liv said. After she'd had more time to develop her career, and of course she would prefer to be married first. Would William be that man? Would she settle out of fear that she would never get another chance? Or would she take a chance and maybe meet a man she loved, and who loved her back? One who looked at her with love and affection and pride, the way Chris looked at Melissa. Didn't she deserve that, too?

If she never married and had kids, would it be that big of a tragedy? She always had her work.

"I love kids," Louisa said. "I'd like at least six, maybe eight."

"Which is why when you meet men, they run screaming in the opposite direction," Anne quipped, but her jab didn't seem to bother her sister.

"The right man is out there," Louisa said, with a tranquil smile and a confidence that suggested she had no doubt. She was probably right. What man wouldn't want to marry a sweet, beautiful princess? Even if it meant having an entire brood of children.

"We all know that Aaron doesn't want kids," Anne said, shooting Liv a meaningful look.

Did she suspect that something was going on between Liv and her brother? And if so, did she honestly believe that Liv would consider him as a potential father to her children? Nothing could be further from the truth. If they did have a fling, which was a moot point because she had already decided they wouldn't, she would never expect more than a brief affair.

Unsure of how to react, Liv decided it was best to give her no reaction at all and instead studied her cards.

"I'm just not cut out to be a family man," Aaron said to no one in particular. If he caught the meaning of his sister's statement, he didn't let on. Or maybe he was saying it for Liv's benefit, just in case she was having any delusions of grandeur and thought they had some sort of future together.

"You would have to drop out of the girl-of-the-month club," Anne said with a rueful smile and a subtle glance in Liv's direction.

"And miss out on that fantastic yearly rate they give me?" Aaron said with a grin. "I think not."

"Are we going to talk or play?" Chris complained, which, to Liv's profound relief, abruptly ended the conversation.

Louisa tried occasionally to engage them in conversation, earning a stern look from her oldest brother each time. She finally gave up and said good-night around ten. Half an hour later Melissa followed. At eleven-thirty, when Liv was up by almost two hundred euros, they packed it in for the night.

"Good game," Chris said, shaking her hand, and added with a grin, "I hope you'll give us a chance to win our money back next week."

"Of course," she said, although she would have to throw the game to make it happen.

"I'll walk you to your room," Aaron said, gesturing to the door, and he had a curious, almost sly look on his face. Something was definitely up.

"Why are you looking at me like that?" she asked.

"Because we finally get some time alone."

Ten

The idea of being alone with Aaron again both terrified and thrilled Liv, then he went and added another level of tension by saying, "You do realize that counting cards is considered cheating."

Oh damn.

She really hadn't thought anyone was paying that close attention. They were playing for only a couple hundred euros, so what was the harm?

She plastered on a look of pure innocence that said, *Me? Cheat?* But she could see he wasn't buying it.

She sighed and said, "It's not my fault."

He raised one disbelieving brow at her.

"I don't even do it consciously. The numbers just kind of stick in my head."

"You have a photographic memory?"

She nodded.

"I wondered how you managed to memorize the code for the lab door so quickly. Although for the life of me I don't understand how you kept getting lost in the castle."

"It only works with numbers."

For a second she though he might be angry, but he shot her a wry smile instead. "At least you made a bit of money for your research."

He apparently had no idea of the going rate for genetic research. "A couple hundred euros won't get me very far."

"You mean thousand," he said.

"Excuse me?"

"A couple hundred thousand."

She nearly tripped on her feet and went tumbling down the stairs. "That's not even funny."

He shrugged. "I'm not trying to be funny."

"You're serious?"

"*Totally* serious."

"You said we were starting with one hundred."

"We did. One hundred thousand."

She suddenly felt weak in the knees. All this time she thought she'd been betting a dollar or ten, it had actually been thousands? What if she'd lost? How would she have ever paid her debt?

"I'll give the money back," she said.

"That would look suspicious. Besides," he reminded her, "you already told Chris you would play again next Friday."

Damn it, she had, hadn't she? If the rest of the family figured it out, they might think her some sort of con artist. Next week she would just have to lose on purpose, claim that her first time must have been beginner's luck, then pretend to be discouraged and vow never to play again. Only she and Aaron would know the truth.

When they reached her room she opened the door and stepped inside. A single lamp burned beside the bed and the covers had been turned down. Standing in the doorway, she turned to him and said, "I had fun tonight."

He leaned against the doorjamb, wearing that devilish, adorable grin. "Aren't you going to invite me in?"

"No."

"Why not?"

"I told you earlier, we can't be…intimate." Just saying the word made her cheeks flush.

"You said it, but we both know you didn't mean it." He leaned in closer. "You want me, Liv."

She did. So much that she ached. He smelled so good and looked so damn sexy wearing that wicked, playful smile, and he was emitting enough phero-mones to make any woman bend to his will.

"That doesn't make it right," she told him, but

with a pathetic degree of conviction. She didn't even believe herself.

Which was probably why, instead of saying goodnight and closing the door in his face, Liv grabbed the front of his shirt, pulled him into her room and kissed him.

He reacted with a surprised, "Oomf," which she had to admit gave her a decadent feeling of power. But it took him only seconds to recover, then he was kissing her back, pulling her into his arms. He shut the door and walked her backward to the bed, tugging the hem of her shirt free from the waist of her pants. She did the same to him, their arms getting tangled. They broke the kiss so that they could pull the shirts over their heads, and the sight of his bare chest took her breath away. He didn't even seem put off by her very plain and utilitarian cotton bra. His eyes raked over her, heavy with lust, and when his hands settled on her bare skin, she shuddered. He was so beautiful, so perfect, she could hardly believe it was real. That he wanted someone like her.

It's just sex, she reminded herself, although deep down, it felt like more.

He tugged the band from her hair and it spilled down around her bare shoulders.

"You're beautiful," he said, looking as though he sincerely meant it. She wished she could see what he saw, see herself through his eyes for one night.

He lowered his head, brushing his lips against the

crest of one breast, just above the cup of her bra. She shuddered again and curled her fingers through his hair.

"You smell fantastic," he said, then he ran his tongue where his lips had just been, up one side and down the other, and a moan slipped from between her lips. "Taste good, too," he added with a devilish grin.

"What are we doing?" she asked.

He regarded her curiously. "As a scientist, I'd have thought someone would have explained it to you by now."

She couldn't help but smile. "I know *what* we're doing. I just don't understand *why*."

"I don't know what you mean."

"Why me?"

She expected him to tease her, to tell her that she was underestimating herself again; instead his expression was serious.

"Honestly, I'm not sure." He caressed her cheek with the backs of his fingers. "All I know is, I've never wanted a woman the way I want you."

She might have suspected it was a line, but his eyes told her that he was telling the truth. That he was just as stunned and confused by this unlikely connection as she was.

Then he kissed her and started touching her, and she didn't care why they were doing it, her only thought was how wonderful his hands felt on her skin, how warm and delicious his mouth felt as he tasted and nipped her. With a quick flick of his fingers he unhooked her bra, and as he bared her breasts, he didn't seem to notice or care how voluptuous she wasn't, and as he drew one nipple into his mouth, flicking lightly with his tongue, she didn't care, either. He made her feel beautiful and desirable.

There was this burning need inside her like she'd never felt before, a sweet ache between her thighs that made her want to beg him to touch her, but he was still concentrating all of his efforts above her waist—and it was driving her mad.

Thinking it might move things along, she ran her hand down his chest to his slacks, sliding her fingers along his waistline, just below the fabric, then she moved her hand over his zipper, sucking in a surprised breath when she realized how long and thick he felt. She should have expected that he would be perfect everywhere.

She gave his erection a gentle squeeze and he groaned against her cleavage.

He reached behind him and she wasn't sure what he was doing, until he tossed his wallet down on the mattress. Intelligent as she was, it took her several seconds to understand why, and when she did—when she realized that he kept his condoms in there—the reality of what they were doing and exactly where this was leading hit her full force.

The fading flower who in college wouldn't even let a man kiss her until the third date was about to have sex with a man she'd known only four days. A playboy prince who without a doubt was far more experienced than she could ever hope to be.

So why wasn't she afraid, or at least a little wary? Why did it just make her want him that much more?

"Take them off," he told her, his voice husky.

She gazed up at him, confused. Only when she saw the look on his face did she realize how aroused he was, and that she was rhythmically stroking him without even realizing it. Reacting solely on instinct.

"My pants," he said. "Take them off now."

With trembling fingers she fumbled with the clasp, then pulled down the zipper. She tugged the slacks down, leaving his boxers in place.

"All of it," he demanded, so she pulled the boxers down, too. "Now, do that again."

She knew what he wanted. He wanted her to touch him again. She took him in her hand and the skin was so hot, she nearly jerked her arm back. Instead she squeezed.

The point of touching him, or at least, part of the point, had been so that he would touch her, too, but so far he was the one getting all of the action. With that thought came a sudden jab of concern that he was one of *those* men. The kind who took pleasure and gave nothing in return. She'd never been with a man who had taken the time to even try to please her, so what made her think Aaron would be any different?

Before she could even complete the thought, Aaron clasped her wrist to stop her. "That feels too good."

Wasn't that the point?

But she didn't argue because he *finally* reached down to unfasten her chinos—much more deftly than she'd managed with his. He eased her pants and panties down together and she kicked them away.

"Lie down," he said, nodding toward the bed. She did as he asked, trembling with anticipation. But instead of lying down beside her, he knelt between her thighs. If she had been more experienced with men, or more to the point, with men like *him*, she probably would have known what was coming next. Instead it was a total surprise when he eased her thighs open, leaned forward and kissed her there. She was so surprised, she wasn't sure what to do, how to react. Then he pressed her legs even farther apart and flicked her with his tongue. The sensation was so shockingly intimate and intense she cried out and arched off the bed. He teased her with his tongue, licking just hard enough to drive her mad, to make her squirm and moan. When she didn't think she could stand much more he took her into his mouth and every muscle from head to toe locked and shuddered in ecstasy, sending her higher and higher, and when it became too much, too intense, she pushed his head away.

She lay there with her eyes closed, too limp to do more than breathe. She felt the bed shift, and the warmth of Aaron's body beside hers. She pried her eyes open to find him grinning down at her. "Everything all right?"

It took all of her energy to nod. "Oh, yeah."

"Are you always that fast?"

"I have no idea."

"What do you mean."

"No man has actually ever done that."

He frowned. "Which part?"

"Either. Both. The few men I've been with weren't exactly…adventurous. And they were more interested in their own pleasure than mine."

"Are you saying no man has ever given you an orgasm?"

"Nope."

"That's just…*wrong*. There's nothing more satisfying for me than giving a woman pleasure."

"Really?" She didn't think it worked that way. Or maybe he was in a class all by himself.

"And you know the best part?" he said.

"Huh?"

He grinned that wolfish smile. "I get to spend the rest of the night proving it to you."

In his life Aaron had never been with a woman so responsive or easy to satisfy as Liv. She climaxed so quickly, and so often, just using his hands and mouth, that it sort of took the challenge out of it. But the way he looked at it, he was helping her make up for lost time. Those other men she'd been with must have been totally inept, completely self-absorbed or just plain stupid. That gave all men a bad rap. He'd never seen anything as fantastic as Liv shuddering in ecstasy, eyes blind with satisfaction.

"I want you inside me," she finally pleaded, gazing up at him with lust-filled eyes, and he couldn't resist giving her exactly what she wanted. He grabbed a condom and tore the package open with his teeth. He looked down at Liv and realized she was staring at his hard-on with a look on her face that hovered somewhere between curiosity and fascination.

"Can I do it?" she asked, holding out her hand.

He shrugged and gave her the condom. "Knock yourself out."

He expected her to roll it on; instead she leaned forward and took him in her mouth. Deep in her mouth. He groaned and wound his hands through her hair, on the verge of an explosion.

She took him from her mouth, looked up at him and grinned.

"I figured it would go on better this way. Besides, I've always wanted to try that."

She could experiment on him anytime. And he truly hoped she would.

He gritted his teeth as she carefully rolled the condom down the length of him.

"Like that?" she asked.

"Perfect," he said, and before he could make another move she lay back, pulling him down on top of her, between her thighs, arching to accept him.

She was so hot and wet and *tight* that he nearly lost

it on the first thrust. And though he was determined to make it last, she wasn't making it easy. Her hands were all over him, threading through his hair, her nails clawing at his back and shoulders, and she wrapped those gloriously long legs around his waist, whimpering in his ear. Then she tensed and moaned and her body clamped down around him like a fist, and it was all over. They rode it out together, then lay gasping for breath, a tangle of arms and legs.

"I had no idea it could be like this," she said.

Neither did he. "You say that as if we're done."

She rose up on one elbow and looked down at him, her expression serious. "I can't marry William."

"That's what I keep telling you," he said. He just hoped she hadn't decided to set her sights on him instead. They had fantastic sexual chemistry, but that didn't change the fact that he had every intention of remaining a free man. William wasn't the right man for her, but neither was he.

"If I wanted to marry him, I would feel guilty right now, wouldn't I?"

"I would think so."

"I don't. Not at all. In fact I almost feel…*relieved*. Like this huge weight has been lifted from my shoulders."

"That's good, right?"

She nodded. "I'm not ready to get married. And even if I was, I can't marry a man I don't love, that I'm not even sexually attracted to. I want more than that."

"You deserve more."

"I do," she agreed, looking as though, for the first time in her life, she finally believed it. "We have to keep this quiet."

"About William?"

"No. About us. Unless…" She frowned.

"Unless what?"

"Well, maybe we shouldn't do this again."

"Don't you think that's a bit unrealistic? Since you got here we haven't been able to keep our hands off each other."

"Then we'll have to be very discreet. Anne already suspects something."

He shrugged. "So what?"

"I'm going to go out on a limb here and assume that your family wouldn't approve of you slumming it with the hired help."

"You're a *guest*," he reminded her. "Besides, I don't give a damn what my family thinks."

"But I do. I spent most of my life trying not to be one of *those* girls. Having sex for the sake of sex."

"This is different."

"Is it really?"

He wanted to say yes, but they were by definition having an affair. And although he hated to admit it, if he were sleeping with a woman of his own social level, his siblings wouldn't bat an eyelash. Liv's humble beginnings and lack of pedigree put her in an entirely different category.

Even though *he* didn't think of her any differently than a duchess or debutante, she was probably right in believing other people would.

It wasn't fair, but it was just the way the world worked. No point in making this any more complicated than necessary.

"They won't hear a word about it from me," he told her.

"Thank you."

"Now," he said with a grin, "where were we?" He pulled her down for a kiss, but just as their lips met, his cell phone began to ring. "Ignore it."

"What if it's something about your father?"

She was right of course. He mumbled a curse and leaned over the edge of the bed to grab it from the floor. He looked at the display and saw that it was Chris. He answered with an irritated, "What?"

"Sorry to wake you, but we need you in the security office."

He didn't tell him that he hadn't been sleeping. And that he had no intention of sleeping for quite some time. He and Liv weren't even close to being finished. "It can't wait until morning?"

"Unfortunately, no. Besides, you wouldn't want to pass up the opportunity to say I told you so."

Eleven

The Gingerbread Man, as he liked to call himself, was back in business.

Posing as hospital housekeeping staff, he'd made it as far as the royal family's private waiting room. Hours after he was gone, security found the chilling calling card he'd left behind. An envelope full of photographs of Aaron and his siblings that the Gingerbread Man had taken in various places. The girls shopping in Paris, and one of Chris taken through the office window of a building where he'd recently had a meeting with local merchants. Every shot of Aaron showed him with a different woman.

It wasn't a direct threat, but the implication was

clear. He was watching them, and despite all of their security, they were vulnerable. And either he'd gotten bolder or he'd made a critical error, because he'd let himself be caught on the hospital surveillance. Aaron stood in the security office with Chris watching the grainy image from the surveillance tape.

"How in the hell did he get so close to the king?" Aaron asked.

"His ID checked out," Randal Jenkins, their head of security, told him. "He must have either stolen a badge from another employee or fabricated one. He never actually looks up at the camera, so he may be difficult to identify."

"We need to tighten down security at the hospital," Chris told him.

"Already done, sir."

"The king knows?" Aaron asked.

"He and the queen were informed immediately as a precaution," Jenkins said. "The London police are involved, as well. They're talking with the hospital staff to see if anyone remembers him, and they're suggesting we take the news public, run the security tape on television in hope that someone will recognize him."

"What do you think?" Aaron asked his brother. "Personally, I'd like to see this lunatic behind bars, but it's your call."

"Take it to the public," Chris told Jenkins. "And until we catch him, no one will leave the castle without a full security detail, and we'll limit any un-necessary travel or personal appearances."

"That will be difficult with the holidays approaching," Aaron said. "Christmas is barely a month away."

"I'm confident that by then he'll be in custody," Chris said.

Aaron wished he shared that confidence, but he had the feeling that it wouldn't be that easy.

Though Aaron assured her that the king was fine and it was nothing more than a security issue that needed his attention, Liv tossed and turned, sleeping fitfully. She roused at 5:00 a.m. so completely awake that she figured she might as well get to work.

The castle was still dark and quiet, but the kitchen was bustling with activity.

"Getting an early start, miss?" Geoffrey asked, sounding almost...friendly.

"I couldn't sleep," she told him.

"Shall I bring you coffee?"

Was he actually being *nice* to her? "Yes, please. If it's no trouble."

He nodded. "I'll be down shortly."

Liv headed down the stairs, grinning like an idiot. Though it shouldn't have mattered what Geoffrey thought of her, she couldn't help but feel accepted somehow, as if she'd gained access to the secret club.

As she rounded the corner to the lab door, she stopped abruptly and the smile slipped from her face.

She distinctly remembered turning out the lights last night before going up for dinner. Now they were blazing. The assistant, a mousy young girl from the university, didn't have a code for the door. As far as Liv knew, no one but herself, Aaron, Geoffrey and the security office had access, and she couldn't imagine what business they might have down there.

She approached the door cautiously, peering through the window. As far as she could see, there was no one there. So why did she have the eerie sensation she was being watched?

"Problem, miss?"

Liv screeched with surprise and spun around, her backpack flying off her shoulder and landing with a thud on the ground. Geoffrey stood behind her carrying a tray with her coffee.

She slapped a hand over her frantically beating heart. "You scared me half to death!"

"Something wrong with the door?" he inquired, looking mildly amused, the first real emotion she had ever seen him show.

"Do you know if anyone was down here last night?" she asked.

"Not that I'm aware of." He stepped past her and punched in his code. The door clicked open and he stepped inside. Liv grabbed her backpack and cautiously followed him.

"I know I turned out the lights when I left last night, but they were on when I came down."

"Maybe you forgot." He set the coffee down on the table beside her desk.

When she saw the surface of her desk, she gasped.

He turned, regarding her curiously. "Something wrong, miss?"

"My desk," she said. The papers and files that had been strewn everywhere were now all stacked in neat piles. "Someone straightened it."

"They're just trying to get your attention," he said, pouring her a cup of coffee.

"Who?" Had someone been snooping down there?

"The spirits."

Spirits?

She had to resist rolling her eyes. It surprised her that a man as seemingly logical as the butler would buy in to that otherwordly garbage. "I don't believe in ghosts."

"All the more reason for them to ruffle your feathers. But you needn't worry, they're perfectly harmless."

It would explain how the door kept opening on its own, when security claimed the log had shown no record of the keypad being used, and maintenance had found nothing amiss with the controls. Yet she still believed it was far more likely that someone was messing with her head or trying to frighten her. Maybe even Geoffrey?

But why?

"Shall I call you for breakfast?" Geoffrey asked.

"I think I'll skip it," she said.

Geoffrey nodded politely, then let himself out of the lab.

Liv wasn't exactly looking forward to facing Aaron's family again. What if someone else had figured out how she'd done so well at poker? Or even worse, what if they knew Aaron had been in her room last night?

If it were possible, she would stay holed up in her lab until the day she was able to go home to the States.

She took her computer out of her backpack and booted it up. As she did every morning, she checked her e-mail first and among the usual spam the filter always missed, she was surprised to find a message from William. There was no subject, and the body of the e-mail said simply, *Just checking your progress.* That was it. Nothing personal like, *How are you?* Or, *Have you made a decision yet?*

She was going to have to tell him that she couldn't marry him. Let him down easy. She would be honest and explain that she just wasn't ready to marry anyone yet, and hope that it wouldn't affect their friendship or their working relationship.

But she couldn't do it through e-mail; that would be far too impersonal, and she hadn't yet worked up the nerve to call him. Maybe it would be better if she waited until she flew home and did it face-to-face.

But was it really fair to string him along? If he knew what she'd been up to last night…

A pleasant little shiver tingled through her body

when she recalled the way Aaron had touched her last night. The way he'd driven her mad with his hands and his mouth. Just thinking about it made her feel warm all over. Even though deep down something was telling her that she would end up regretting it, that she was way out of her league and headed for imminent disaster, she could hardly wait to be alone with him again.

Maybe last night was a total fluke and the next time they had sex it would only be so-so, even though she doubted it. If she kept thinking about it, about *him,* she wouldn't get a thing done today.

She answered William's mail with an equally impersonal rundown of her progress so far, and asked him to please go over the data she planned to send him later that afternoon—a fresh eye never hurt—then she got back to work analyzing the samples her assistant had taken yesterday.

Although she usually became engrossed in her work, she couldn't shake the feeling that she was being watched, and kept looking over to the door. The window wasn't more than ten-by-ten inches square, but a few times she could swear she saw the shadow of a figure just outside. Was it possible that Aaron or one of his siblings had someone keeping an eye on her? What did they think she might be doing down there, other than saving their country from agricultural devastation?

Or maybe it was just her mind playing tricks.

Some time later she heard the sound of the door clicking open, and thought, Here we go again. She was relieved when she heard footsteps moving in her direction. Assuming it was probably Geoffrey fetching the empty coffee carafe, she paid no attention, until she felt a rush of cool air brush past her and the unmistakable weight of a hand on her shoulder. She realized it had to be Aaron, there to say good morning. She pried herself away from her computer and spun in her chair to smile up at him, but there was no one there. She looked over at the door and saw that it was still firmly closed.

She shot to her feet and an eerie shiver coursed through her. It had to be her imagination. Could she have dozed off for a second? Maybe dreamed it?

If she had been sleeping, she wouldn't feel completely awake and alert. She glanced back up at the door and saw distinct movement outside the window, then it clicked and swung open. She sat there frozen, expecting some ghoulish apparition to float through, relieved when it was Aaron who stepped into the lab.

Her apprehension must have shown because when he saw her standing there, he stopped in his tracks and frowned. "You look as though you've just seen a ghost."

"Do you have someone spying on me?"

Taken aback by Liv's question, Aaron said, "Good morning to you, too."

"I'm serious, Aaron. Please tell me the truth."

Not only did she look serious, but deeply disturbed by the possibility. How could she even ask him that? "Of course not."

"You mean it?"

"Liv, if I felt you needed constant supervision, I never would have invited you here."

"Could your brother or one of your sisters have someone watching me?"

"I can't imagine why they would."

She shuddered and hugged herself. "This is too weird."

He walked over to her desk. "What's wrong?"

"I keep getting this feeling like someone is watching me, and when I look up at the window in the door, I see a shadow, like someone is standing just outside."

"Maybe someone on the laundry staff has a crush on you," he joked, but she didn't look amused. "I don't know who it could be."

"You know that the door kept popping open yesterday, and the technician said there wasn't anything wrong with it. Then this morning when I came down here, the lights were on and I know I turned them off last night."

He shrugged. "Maybe you thought you did, but didn't hit the switch all the way or something."

"Then explain how the papers that were strewn all over my desk were stacked neatly this morning."

He frowned. "Okay, that is kind of weird."

"There's something else."

"What?"

She looked hesitant to tell him, but finally said, "This is going to sound completely crazy, but a few minutes before you came in I heard the door open and footsteps in the room, then someone touched my shoulder, but when I turned around no one was there and the door was closed."

He might have thought it was crazy, but he'd heard similar stories from the staff. "Lots of people have reported having strange experiences down here."

"I don't believe in ghosts," she said, but without a whole lot of conviction. "Scientific labs aren't typically hot spots for paranormal activity."

"But how many labs have you been in that used to be dungeons?"

"None," she admitted.

"If it eases your mind, no one has ever been physically harmed down here. Just frightened."

"I don't feel as though I'm in physical danger. It's just creepy to think that someone is watching me. And—" she shuddered again "—*touching* me."

"Do you want to leave?"

"You mean, permanently?"

He nodded. God knows he didn't want her to; they needed her expertise and would be hard-pressed to find someone equally qualified, but he would understand if she had to.

"Of course not," she said, and he felt a little too relieved for comfort.

He tried to tell himself that he was only concerned

for his country's welfare, but he knew that was nonsense. He wanted more time with Liv. At least a few weeks to get her out of his system.

He grinned and told her, "I guess that means I'll just have to protect you."

He wrapped a hand around her hip and tugged her to him. She resisted for about half a second, then gave in and melted into his arms, resting her head on his shoulder. She felt so warm and soft and she smelled delicious. If they weren't in the lab, he would already be divesting her of her clothing.

"I had fun last night," he said and he could swear he felt her blush.

She wrapped her arms around him and hugged herself to his chest. "Me, too. Did you resolve your security problem?"

"In a manner of speaking." Because it wasn't a secret, and she would eventually be informed of the security lockdown, he figured he might as well tell her about the Gingerbread Man.

"That's really creepy," she said, gazing up at him. "Why would someone want to hurt your family?"

Aaron shrugged. "There are a lot of crazy people out there."

"I guess."

He kissed the tip of her nose. "I didn't think I'd find you in the lab. I figured, because it's the weekend, you might not be working today. I thought you might be up to a game of billiards."

"I work every day."

"Even Sunday?"

She gazed up at him and nodded. "Even Sunday."

"That reminds me. Chris wanted to know how long you'll need for the holidays."

She looked confused. "Need for what?"

"To go home."

"Oh, I won't be going home. I don't celebrate Christmas."

"Why not?" he asked, thinking that maybe it was some sort of religious issue.

She shrugged. "No one to celebrate with, I guess."

He frowned. "You must have friends."

"Yes, but they all have families and I would feel out of place. It really is not a big deal."

But it was. It was a very big deal. The thought of her spending the holidays alone disturbed him in a way he hadn't expected. It made him...*angry*. If her so-called friends really cared about her, they would insist she spend the holidays with them.

"If you're worried about me getting in the way, I'll keep to myself," she assured him. "You won't even know I'm here."

What kind of person did she think him to be? "That is the most ridiculous thing I've ever heard," he said, and she looked startled by his sharp tone. "I won't let you spend Christmas alone. You'll celebrate with us."

"Aaron, I don't think—"

"This is *not* negotiable. I'm *telling* you. You're spending the holidays with my family."

She opened her mouth to argue, so he did the only thing he could to shut her up. He leaned forward, covered her lips with his and kissed her.

Twelve

Aaron was making it really difficult for her to tell him no. Literally. Every time they came up for air, and she would open her mouth to speak, he would just start kissing her again. She was beginning to feel all soft and mushy-brained and turned on. Yet she couldn't shake the feeling they were being watched.

She opened one eye and peered at the door, nearly swallowing her own tongue when she saw a face staring back at her through the window. A woman she didn't recognize, with long, curly blond hair wearing some sort of lacy bonnet. Liv's first thought was that someone had discovered their secret, and they were both in big trouble. Then before her eyes the face went misty and translucent and seemed to dissipate and disappear into thin air.

She let out a muffled shriek against Aaron's lip, then ripped herself free so fast that she stumbled backward, tripped over her chair and landed on her rear end on the hard linoleum floor.

"Bloody hell, what's wrong?" Aaron asked, stunned by her sudden outburst.

She pointed to the door, even though whoever, or *whatever,* she'd seen in the window was no longer there. "A f-face."

He spun around to look. "There's no one there."

"It disappeared."

"Whoever it was probably saw you looking and ran off."

"No. I mean, it actually disappeared. One minute it was there, and the next minute it vanished. I don't even know how to explain it. It was as if it...dissolved."

"Dissolved?"

"Like mist." It was scary as hell, but the scientist in her couldn't help feeling intrigued. She had always clung to the belief that there was no such thing as heaven or an afterlife. When you were dead, you were dead. Could this mean there was some sort of life after death?

He looked at the window again, then back to her, still sprawled on the floor. "Are you saying that you saw a ghost?"

"A few days ago I never would have believed it,

but I can't think of any other logical explanation." And for some reason, seeing it with her own eyes, knowing it was real, made her more curious than frightened. She wanted to see it again.

He held out a hand to help her up, and when she was on her feet he tugged her back into his arms. "If someone was watching us, alive or otherwise, they nearly got one hell of a view, because I was about two seconds from ravishing you."

So much for being discreet. "Suppose someone on this plane of existence did happen to come down and look in the window?"

"So we'll cover it," he said, nibbling on her neck. "A sheet of paper and some tape should do the trick."

What he was doing felt deliciously wonderful, but now wasn't the time for fooling around. Although she had the feeling that when it came to women, he was used to getting his way. If he was going to be with her, he was going to have to learn to compromise.

"Aaron, I have to work," she said firmly, planting her hands on his chest.

"No, you don't," he mumbled against her skin.

She gave a gentle but firm shove. "Yes. *I do*."

He hesitated a moment, then grudgingly let her go. "Do I get to see you at all today?"

Though she could easily work late into the evening, if he had to compromise, then so should she. "How about a game of billiards tonight after dinner?"

He grinned. "And after billiards?"

She just smiled.

"I'm holding you to it," he said, backing toward the door.

"Oh, and about Christmas," she said.

"It's not up for discussion."

"But your family—"

"Won't mind at all. Besides, if Melissa were to get wind of you spending the holidays alone, she would probably have an emotional meltdown."

He was probably right. If Aaron didn't insist she join them, Melissa probably would. Or maybe she was rationalizing.

Compromise, Liv. Compromise.

"Okay," she said, and that seemed to make him very happy.

"See you at dinner," he said as he walked out.

She'd never had what anyone would consider a conventional Christmas holiday. Her foster families never had money for gifts and extravagant meals. If she got candy in her stocking—hell, if she even *had* a stocking—it was a pretty good year. It used to make her sad when the kids at school returned after the holiday break sporting new clothes and handheld video games and portable CD players, but she'd learned to harden her heart.

Even now Christmas was just another day to her. But she would be lying if she said it didn't get a *little* lonely, knowing everyone else was with their families.

But there were definite benefits, too. She didn't

have to fight the holiday crowds shopping for gifts, or have outrageous credit card bills come January. The simpler she kept her life, the better. Although it might be a nice change to spend Christmas somewhere other than alone in the lab. With a real family.

Or maybe, she thought as she sat down in front of her computer, it would make her realize all that she'd been missing.

Liv fidgeted beside Aaron as they neared the king's suite. His parents had returned from England yesterday, several days later than expected due to mild complications caused by the reinsertion of the pump. But he was feeling well, in good spirits and happy to be home with his family.

"Maybe we shouldn't bother them," Liv said, her brow furrowed. "I'm sure the king needs rest."

"He *wants* to meet you," he assured her. She'd grown much more comfortable in the castle this past week. She seemed to enjoy spending time with his siblings, and the feeling was remarkably mutual. Even Anne had lowered her defenses within the past few days and seemed to be making a genuine effort to get to know Liv, and of course Louisa loved everyone.

He took Liv's hand and gave it a reassuring squeeze, and even though no one was around, she pulled from his grasp. He was breaking her rule of no public displays of affection. Although he was quite sure that if his siblings hadn't already begun to suspect their affair, it was only a matter of time. Nearly every moment Liv wasn't in the lab, Aaron was with her and he'd spent every night for the past seven days in her room.

If they did suspect, no one had said a word to him.

"I'm so nervous. I'm afraid that when I curtsy I'm going to fall on my face."

"If you fall, I'll catch you," he assured her. He knocked on the suite door then pushed it open, feeling Liv go tense beside him.

His father had dressed for the occasion, though he was reclined on the sofa. His mother rose to greet them as they entered the room.

"Liv, meet my parents, the King and Queen of Thomas Isle. Mother, Father, this is Olivia Montgomery."

Liv curtsied, and even though it wasn't the smoothest he'd ever seen, she was nowhere close to falling over.

"It's an honor to meet you both," she said, a slight quiver in her voice.

"The honor is all ours, Miss Montgomery," his father said, shaking her hand, which she did gingerly, Aaron noticed, as though she worried she might break him. "Words cannot express how deeply we appreciate your visit."

His mother didn't even offer to shake Liv's hand. Maybe the king's health and all that time in the hospital was taking its toll on her. Although she'd seemed fine yesterday. Just a bit tired.

"My children speak quite highly of you," the king said, and added with a grin, "in fact, I hear you're something of a card shark."

Liv smiled nervously. "I'm sure it was beginner's luck, Your Highness."

"I'm assuming you've had time to work since you arrived," his mother said and her curt tone took him aback.

Liv looked a little stunned as well, so Aaron answered, "Of course she has. I practically have to drag her out of the lab just to eat dinner. She would work around the clock if I didn't insist she take a break every now and then."

She ignored him and asked Liv in an almost-demanding tone, "Have you made any progress?"

As was the case when she talked about her work or someone questioned her professionally, she suddenly became the confident and assertive scientist. The transformation never ceased to amaze him.

"I'm very close to discovering the strain of disease affecting the crops," she told his mother. Usually she explained things to him in layman's terms, so he had at least a little hope of understanding what she was talking about. She must have been trying to make a point because when she explained her latest developments to his mother, she used all scientific terms and jargon. Though the queen had spent the better part of her life farming, botanical genetics was *way* out of her league.

By the time Liv finished with her explanation, his mother looked at least a little humbled.

"Would you mind excusing us, Miss Montgomery," the queen said. "I need to have a word with my son."

"Of course," Liv said. "I need to get back down to the lab anyway. It was a pleasure to meet you both."

"I'll walk you out," Aaron said, leading her from the room.

When they were in the hallway with the door closed, Liv turned to him and said, "I'm so sorry."

Her apology confused him. He should be the one apologizing for his mother's behavior. "For what? I thought you were fantastic."

She frowned, looking troubled. "I was showing off. It was rude of me."

"Love, you've earned the right to show off every now and then."

"Your mother hates me."

"Why would she hate you?"

"Because she knows."

He frowned. "Knows what?"

She lowered her voice, even though they were alone. "That something is going on between us."

"How could she?"

"I don't know, but that was a mother lion protecting her cub. Her message clearly said back off."

"You're being paranoid. I think between my

father's health, the security breach at the hospital and the diseased crops, she's just stressed out."

Liv didn't look as though she believed him, but she didn't push the issue.

"I'll come see you in the lab later." He brushed a quick kiss across her lips, ignoring her look of protest, then let himself back into his parents' suite. He crossed the room to where they still sat, determined to get to the bottom of this.

"What the bloody hell was that about?" he asked his mother.

"Watch your tone," his father warned.

"*My* tone? Could she have been any more rude to Liv?"

"Don't think I don't know what's going on between you two," his mother said.

So Liv had been right. She did suspect something. He folded his arms over his chest. "And what *is* going on, Mother?"

"Nothing that your father and I approve of."

"You haven't even been here, so how could you possibly know what's been going on? Do you have the staff watching me?"

"There's someone I want you to meet," she said. "She's a duchess from a *good* family."

Unlike Liv who had *no* family, was that what she meant? That was hardly Liv's fault. "If you're concerned that I'm going to run off and marry Liv, you can stop worrying."

"It isn't proper. She's not of noble blood."

If his mother had the slightest clue about the behavior of those so-called *proper* women she set him up with, she would have kittens. The spoiled brats whose daddies gave them everything their hearts desired, while they dabbled in drugs and alcohol, and were more often than not sexually promiscuous. Liv was a saint in comparison.

"Maybe you should take the time to know her before you pass judgment."

"I know all I need to. She's not good enough for you," his mother said.

"Not *good* enough? I can safely say she's more intelligent than all three of us combined. She's sweet, and kind, and down-to-earth. And she could very well be saving our *asses* from total financial devastation," he said, earning a stern look from his father. "Can you say that of your princesses or duchesses?"

"The decision has already been made," his mother said. "You'll meet the duchess next Friday."

Since Chris married Melissa, their mother had been determined to find Aaron a wife, and even though he'd told her a million times he didn't want to settle down, the message seemed to go in one ear and out the other. But he'd gone along with the blind dates and the setups because it was always easier than arguing. Easier than standing up for himself.

He thought of Liv, who had fought like hell for everything she'd ever gotten, how strong she was, and wondered what had he ever done but settle? From the day he was born his family told him who he was supposed to be. Well, he was tired of compromising himself, tired of playing by their rules. It ended today.

"No," he said.

She frowned. "No, what?"

"I won't meet her."

"Of course you will."

"No, I won't. No more blind dates, no more setups. I'm finished."

She huffed out a frustrated breath. "How will you ever find a wife if you don't—"

"I don't *want* a wife. I don't want to settle down."

She rolled her eyes. "Every man says that. But when the right one comes along you'll change your mind."

"If that's true, I'll find her without your help."

She gave him her token you-would-be-lost-without-me-to-run-your-life look. "Aaron, sweetheart—"

"I mean it, Mother. I don't want to hear another word about it."

She looked stunned by his demand; his father, on the other hand, looked amused. "He's made his decision, dear," he said. And before she could argue, he sighed and said, "This conversation has worn me out."

"Why didn't you say something?" She patted his shoulder protectively and summoned the nurse, shooting Aaron a look that suggested his father's sudden fatigue was his fault. "Let's get you to bed. We'll talk about this later."

No, they wouldn't, he wanted to say, but for his father's sake he let it drop. She would come to realize that he wasn't playing by her rules any longer.

While the nurse helped his father into bed, his mother turned to him and said, "Please let Geoffrey know that your father and I will be taking dinner in our suite tonight."

"Of course."

She smiled and patted his cheek fondly. "That's a good boy."

A good boy? Ugh. What was he, twelve? He turned and left before he said something he regretted. She seemed to believe she'd won, but nothing could be further from the truth. Knowing Liv had made him take a good hard look at his own life and he didn't like what he was seeing. It was time he made a few changes.

Thirteen

The following Monday was December first and overnight the castle was transformed to a holiday wonderland. Fresh evergreen swags dotted with red berries and accented with big red bows hung from the stair railings, making everything smell piney and festive, and mistletoe hung in every door and archway. Life-size nutcrackers stood guard in the halls and every room on the main floor had a Christmas tree decorated in a different color and theme. From one hung various styles and flavors of candy canes and other sugar confections, while another was festooned with antique miniature toy ornaments. Some were draped in all shades of purple, and others in creamy whites. But the most amazing tree was in the ballroom. It stood at least twenty feet high, decorated in shimmering silver and gold balls.

The outside of the castle was the most incredible of all. What looked to be about a million tiny multicolored lights edged the windows and turrets and lit the shrubs.

Liv had never seen anything like it, and she couldn't help but get drawn into the holiday spirit. For the first time in her life Christmas wasn't something she dreaded or ignored. This time she let herself feel it, get caught up in the atmosphere. And she almost felt as if she had a family. Aaron's siblings made her feel so welcome, and Liv was particularly fond of the king. He was warm and friendly and had a surprisingly thorough understanding of genetic science and an insatiable curiosity. They had many evening conversations about her research, sitting by the fire in the study sipping hot cider.

"Science is a hobby of mine," he once told her. "As a child I used to dream of being a scientist. I even planned to go to university and study it. That was before I was crown prince."

Much the way Aaron had dreamed of being a doctor, she thought. "You weren't always crown prince?"

"I had an older brother, Edward. He would have been king, but he contracted meningitis when he was fifteen. It left him blind and physically impaired, so the crown was passed on to me. It's a bit ironic, really. We would spend hours in this very room, sitting by the fire. I would read to him, or play his favorite music. And now here I am, the incapacitated one."

"But only temporarily," she reminded him.

He just smiled and said, "Let's hope so."

The queen didn't share her husband's affection for Liv. She wasn't cruel or even rude. She was just…indifferent. Liv had overcome enough adversity in her life to understand that she couldn't let herself be bothered by the opinions of one person, but she would be lying if she said it didn't hurt her feelings just a little. Particularly because she was being judged not on the merits of her accomplishments, or even her morals, but on her lack of pedigree.

The Sunday before Christmas a blizzard dropped nearly a foot of snow and Liv let Aaron talk her into trying cross-country skiing. He wanted to take her to their ski lodge on the other side of the island, but with the Gingerbread Man still on the loose, the king insisted they stay on the castle property.

As Liv anticipated, she spent the better part of the first hour sitting in the snow.

"It just takes practice," Aaron told her as he hauled her back up on her feet again, and she actually managed to make it two or three yards before she fell on her face. But he assured her, "You're doing great!"

As inept as she felt, and embarrassed by her lack of coordination, Aaron's enthusiasm was contagious and she found that she was having fun. Since she arrived on Thomas Isle, he had introduced her to so many things that she otherwise would have never tried. If not for him, she would still be in her lab 24/7, working her life away instead of living it.

As much fun as they had been having, Liv knew it wouldn't last. She was in the process of testing compounds in hope of finding one that would kill the disease, and when she found the right combination, there would be no reason for her to stay. Leaving would be hard because she'd grown attached to Aaron. In fact, she felt she may even be in love with him, but that didn't change who they were. Besides, he had made it quite clear that he didn't want to be tied down. It was destined to end, and all she could do was enjoy the time they had left together.

An hour before sundown, exhausted to the center of her bones and aching in places she didn't even know she could ache, Liv tossed down her poles and said enough.

"You have to admit that was fun," he said as they stripped out of their gear.

"Oh, yeah," she said, hissing in pain as she bent over to unclip the ski boots. "Spending an entire day sitting in the snow has always been my idea of fun."

He shot her a skeptical look.

"Okay," she admitted with a shrug that sent spirals of pain down her back. "Maybe it was a *little* fun."

"You were getting pretty good near the end there."

It was her turn to look skeptical.

"I'm serious," he said. "By the end of winter I'll have you skiing like a pro."

The *end* of winter? How long did he expect her to stay? Did he *want* her to stay? And even more important, did *she* want to?

Of course he didn't. It was just an off-the-cuff remark that he probably hadn't thought through.

They walked up the stairs—well, he walked and she limped—to her room.

"I'm going to dress for dinner," he said. "Shall I pick you up on my way back down?"

"I don't think so."

"Are you sure?"

"Not only am I not hungry, but I'm exhausted and everything hurts. I'd like to lie down for a while."

"I'll come by and check on you later." He brushed a quick kiss across her lips, then headed to his room. She still wasn't comfortable with him showing her physical affection where someone might see. Although she didn't doubt that his family knew what was going on. They had just been kind enough not to say anything. She was sure they saw it for what it was. A fling. But she still didn't feel comfortable advertising it.

She went into her room and limped to the bathroom, downing three ibuprofen tablets before she stepped into the shower. She blasted the water as hot as she could stand, then she toweled off and crawled into bed naked. She must have fallen asleep the instant her head hit the pillow because the next thing she remembered was Aaron sitting on the edge of the mattress.

"What time is it?" she asked, her voice gravelly with sleep.

"Nine." He switched on the lamp beside the bed and she squinted against the sudden flood of light. "How do you feel?"

She tried to move and her muscles screamed in protest. "Awful," she groaned. "Even my eyelids hurt."

"Then you're going to like what I found," he said, holding up a small bottle.

"What is it?"

He flashed her one of his sexy, sizzling smiles. "Massage oil."

He eased back the covers, and when he saw that she was naked, he growled deep in his throat. "I swear, you get more beautiful every day."

He'd told her that so many times, so often that she was beginning to believe him, to see herself through his eyes. And in that instant in time everything was perfect.

He caressed her cheek with the backs of his fingers. "I love…"

Her heart jolted in her chest and she thought for sure that he was going to say he loved her. In that millisecond, she knew without a doubt that her honest reply would be, *I love you, too.*

"…just looking at you," he said instead.

The disappointment she felt was like a crushing weight on her chest, making it difficult to breathe. Tell him you love him, you idiot! But she couldn't do that. Love wasn't part of this arrangement. Instead she didn't say a word, she just wrapped her arms around him and pulled him down for a kiss. And when he made love to her, he was so sweet and gentle that it nearly brought her to tears.

She loved him so fiercely it made her chest ache, and she desperately wanted him to love her, too.

She wasn't sure how much longer she could take this.

It took some convincing on his part, but Aaron talked Liv into another afternoon of skiing on Christmas Eve. And despite her reservations she did exceptionally well. So well that he looked forward to introducing her to other recreational activities, like biking and kayaking and even low-level rock climbing. The problem was, she probably wouldn't be around long enough. He was sorry for that, but in a way relieved. He'd grown closer and more attached to Liv than he had any other woman in his life. Dangerously close. And even though he knew he was walking a very fine and precarious line, he wasn't ready to let go yet.

Christmas morning he woke Liv at 5:45 a.m., despite the fact that they had been up half the night making love.

"It's too early," she groaned, shoving a pillow over her head.

He pulled it back off. "Come on, wake up. We're gathering with everyone in the study at six."

She squinted up at him. "*Six?* What for?"

"To open presents. Then afterward we have a huge breakfast. It's been a tradition as long as I can remember."

She groaned again and closed her eyes. "I'd rather sleep."

"It's *Christmas*. And you promised you would spend it with me and my family, remember?"

"I was thinking that you meant Christmas dinner."

"I meant the entire day." He tugged on her arm. "Now come on, get up."

She grumbled about it, but let him pull her to an upright position. She yawned and rubbed her eyes and asked, "What should I wear?"

"Pajamas." At her questioning look, he added, "It's what everyone else will be wearing."

She made him wait while she brushed her hair and teeth, and when they got to the study his siblings and sister-in-law were already gathered around the tree, waiting to open the piles of gifts stacked there. Their father sat in his favorite armchair and their mother beside him at the hearth. Geoffrey stood at the bar pouring hot cider. Christmas music played softly and a fire blazed in the fireplace.

"Hurry up, you two!" Louisa said excitedly.

"I shouldn't be here," Liv mumbled under her breath, standing stiffly beside him, looking as though she were about to go to the guillotine.

"Of course you should." When she refused to move, he took her hand and pulled her over to the tree and sat her by Louisa. The second she was off her feet she pulled her hand from his.

"Merry Christmas!" Louisa gushed, giving Liv a warm hug, and after a slight hesitation, Liv hugged her back. If anyone could make Liv feel like part of the family, it was Louisa. Although right now she just looked overwhelmed. She looked downright stunned when Anne, who wore the santa hat and passed out the gifts, announced, "And here's one for Olivia from the king and queen."

Liv's jaw actually dropped. "F-for me?"

Anne handed it to her. "That's what the tag says."

She took it and just held it, as if she wasn't sure what to do.

"Aren't you going to open it?" Aaron asked.

"But I didn't get anything for anyone."

His mother surprised him by saying, "Your being here is the only gift we need."

Liv bit her lip, picking gingerly at the taped edge of the paper, while everyone else tore into theirs enthusiastically. It was almost as though she had never opened a gift before or had forgotten how. What disturbed him most was that it might be true. When was the last time anyone had given her anything?

She finally got it open and pulled from the layers of gold tissue paper a deep blue cashmere cardigan.

"Oh," she breathed. "It's beautiful."

"You keep the lab so dreadfully cold," his mother said. "I thought it might come in handy."

"Thank you so much."

Anne passed out another round of gifts and this time there was one for Liv from Chris and Melissa, a pair of thick wool socks.

"For skiing," Melissa told her.

Louisa got Liv a silver bracelet decorated with science-themed charms, and Anne gave her a matching cashmere mitten, scarf and hat set. Aaron had gotten her something, too, but she would have to wait until later to get it.

The last present under the tree was for the king and queen from Chris and Melissa. Their mother opened it and inside was what looked like an ultrasound photo. Did that mean…?

"What is this?" their mother asked, looking confused.

"Those are your grandchildren," Chris said with a grin. "All three of them."

"Three grandchildren!" his mother shrieked, while his father beamed proudly and said, "Congratulations!"

"They implanted five embryos," Melissa said. "Three took. It's still very early, but we couldn't wait to tell you. My doctor said everything looks great."

Aaron had never seen his mother look so proud or

excited. She knelt down to hug them both, then *everyone* was hugging Chris and Melissa and congratulating them.

"Isn't it great? I'm going to be an uncle," Aaron said, turning to Liv, but she wasn't smiling or laughing like the rest of them. In fact, she looked as though she might be sick. "Hey, are you okay?"

She shook her head and said, "Excuse me," then she bolted from the room, seven startled pairs of eyes following her.

"What happened?" his mother asked, and Louisa said, "Did we do something wrong?"

"I don't know," Aaron said, but he was going to find out.

Fourteen

Liv reached her room, heart beating frantically and hands shaking, and went straight to the closet for her suitcase. She dropped it on the bed and opened it just as Aaron appeared in the doorway.

"What happened down there?" he asked, looking concerned. "Are you okay?"

"I'm sorry. Please tell everyone that I'm *so* sorry. I just couldn't take it another minute."

He saw her suitcase and asked, "What are you doing?"

"Packing. I have to leave."

He looked stunned. "Was being with my family really that awful?"

"No, it was absolutely wonderful. I had no idea it could be like that. I just… I can't do this anymore."

"What do you mean? I thought we were having fun."

"I was. I *am*. The time we've spent together has been the best in my life."

She started toward the closet to get her clothes, but he stepped in her way, looking so hopelessly confused she wanted to hug him. "So what's the problem?"

Did he honestly have no idea what was going on? "I know it's illogical and totally irrational, but I've fallen in love with you, Aaron."

She gave him a few seconds to return the sentiment, but he only frowned, looking troubled, and it made her inexplicably sad. She hadn't really believed he would share her feelings, but she had hoped. But as she had reminded herself over and over, the world just didn't work that way. Not the world she lived in.

"We don't have any further to go with this," she said. "And I'm just not the kind of person who can tread water. I think it would be better for us both if I leave now. The work I have left to do, I can finish in my lab in the States."

"You can't leave," he said, looking genuinely upset.

"I have to."

"I *do* care about you."

"I know you do." Just not enough. Not enough for her, anyway. She wanted more. She wanted to be part of a family, to feel as if she belonged somewhere. And not just temporarily. She wanted forever.

She wanted it so badly that she ached, but she would never have that with him.

His brow furrowed. "I just… I can't…"

"I know," she assured him. "This is not your fault. This is *all* me. I never meant to fall in love with you."

"I…I don't know what to say."

Just tell me you love me, she wanted to tell him, but Aaron didn't do love. He didn't get serious and settle down. And even if he did, it wouldn't be with someone like her. She didn't fit in. She wasn't good enough for someone like him.

"I'll pack up the lab today," she told him. "Can you arrange for a flight off the island tomorrow?"

"Won't you at least have dinner with us? It's Christmas."

She shrugged. "It's just another day for me."

That was a lie. It used to be, but after this morning it would forever be a reminder of how wonderful it could be and everything she'd been missing out on, and so *desperately* wanted. In a way she wished she'd never met Aaron, that he'd never called for her help. She would still be living in blissful ignorance.

"You should get back to your family," she told him.

"You're sure I can't convince you to spend the day with us?"

"I'm sure."

He looked disappointed, but he didn't push the issue, and she was relieved because she was this close to caving, to throwing herself into his arms and saying she would stay as long as he wanted. Even if he couldn't love her.

"I'll have Geoffrey bring your gifts up and inform you of your travel arrangements," he said.

"Thank you."

"You're *sure* I can't change your mind?"

There was an almost pleading look in his eyes, and she wanted so badly to give in, but her heart just couldn't take it. "I can't."

"I'll leave you alone to pack."

He stepped out of the room, closing the door behind him, and though it felt so final, she knew she was doing the right thing.

She packed all of her clothes, leaving out one clean outfit for the following day, then she went down to the lab to start packing there, feeling utterly empty inside.

She never had seen the ghost again, but she'd made her presence known by occasionally stacking Liv's papers, hiding her pen or opening the lab door. Maybe she should have felt uncomfortable knowing she wasn't alone, but instead the presence was a comfort. She'd even caught herself talking to her, even though the conversation was always one-sided. She realized now that when she was gone she might even miss her elusive and unconventional companion.

She was going to miss everything about Thomas Isle.

Geoffrey came down around dinnertime with a

plate of food. She wasn't hungry, but she thanked him anyway. "I bet you're happy not to have to deal with me anymore," she joked, expecting him to emphatically agree.

Instead his expression was serious when he said, "Quite the contrary, miss."

She was too stunned to say a word as he turned and left. And here she thought he viewed her as a nuisance. The fact that he hadn't only made her feel worse.

She packed the last of her equipment by midnight, and when she went up to her room, waiting for her as promised were the gifts the family had given her and the itinerary for her trip. She sat down at the desk by the window writing them each a note of thanks, not only for the presents, but for accepting her into their home and treating her like family. She left them on the desk where Elise would find them when she cleaned the room.

She climbed under the covers around one-thirty, but tossed and turned and slept only an hour or two before her alarm buzzed at seven. She got out of bed feeling a grogginess that even a shower couldn't wash away. At seven-forty-five someone came to fetch her luggage, then a few minutes later Flynn from security came to fetch her.

"It's time to go to the airstrip, miss," he said.

"Let's do it," she said, feeling both relieved and heartsick. She wanted so badly to change her mind, to stay just a little bit longer and hope that he would see he loved her. But it was too late to turn back now. Even if it wasn't, she knew in her heart that it would be a bad idea.

She followed Flynn down the stairs to the foyer, and when she saw that the entire family lined up to say goodbye, the muscles in her throat contracted so tight that she could barely breathe. This was the last thing she'd expected. She had assumed her departure would be as uneventful as her arrival.

The king was first in line. If she had expected some cold and formal goodbye, a handshake and a "have a nice life," she couldn't have been more wrong. He hugged her warmly and said, "I've enjoyed our talks."

"Me, too," she said, realizing he was the closest thing she had ever had to a father figure. She hoped with all her being that the heart pump was successful and he lived a long, productive life. Long enough to see his daughters marry and his grandchildren grow. She wasn't a crier, but she could feel the burn of tears in her throat and behind her eyes. All she could manage to squeak out was, "Thanks for everything."

The queen was next. She took Liv's hands and air kissed her cheek. "It's been a pleasure having you with us," she said, and actually looked as though she meant it.

"Thank you for having me in your home," Liv said.

Chris and Melissa stood beside the queen. Chris kissed Liv's cheek and Melissa, with tears running in a steady river down her face—no doubt pregnancy hormones at work—hugged her hard. "Watch the mail for a baby shower invitation. I want you there."

If only. It was a lovely thought, yet totally unrealistic. She was sure by then they would have forgotten all about her.

Louisa scooped her up into a bone-crushing embrace. "We'll miss you," she said. "Keep in touch."

Anne hugged her, too, though not as enthusiastically. But she leaned close and Liv thought she was going to kiss her cheek, but instead she whispered, "My brother is a dolt."

Of all the things anyone could have said to her, that was probably the sweetest, and the tears were hovering so close to the surface now that she couldn't even reply.

Aaron was last, and the one she was least looking forward to saying goodbye to. He stood aside from his family by the door, hands in his pants pockets, eyes to the floor. As she approached he looked up at her.

The tears welled closer to the surface and she swallowed them back down. Please let this be quick and painless.

"You'll contact me when you have results," he said, all business.

She nodded. "Of course. And I'll send you updates on my progress. At the rate it's going, you should have it in plenty of time for the next growing season."

"Excellent." He was quiet for a second, then he said in a low voice, "I'm sorry. I just can't—"

"It's okay," she said, even though it wasn't. Even though it felt as though he was ripping her heart from her chest.

He nodded, looking remorseful. She had started to turn toward the door when he cursed under his breath, hooked a hand behind her neck, pulled her to him and kissed her—*really* kissed her—in front of his entire family. He finally pulled away, leaving her feeling breathless and dizzy, said, "Goodbye Liv," then turned and walked away, taking her heart with him.

The flights to the U.S. couldn't have been smoother or more uneventful, but when Liv got back to her apartment and let herself inside it almost didn't feel like home. She'd barely been gone a month, but it felt as if everything had changed, and there was this nagging ache in the center of her chest that refused to go away.

"You just need sleep," she rationalized.

She climbed into bed and, other than a few trips to the bathroom, didn't get back out for three days. That was when she reminded herself that she'd never been one to wallow in self-pity. She was stronger than that. Besides, she needed to see William. She hadn't spoken to or even e-mailed him in weeks. Maybe they could have a late lunch and talk about his proposal and she could let him down easy.

She tried calling him at the lab, but he wasn't there and he wasn't answering his house or cell phone. Concerned that something might be wrong, she drove to his house instead.

She knocked, then a minute later knocked harder. She was about to give up and leave when the door finally opened.

Being that it was the middle of the afternoon, she was surprised to find him in a T-shirt and pajama bottoms, looking as though he'd just rolled out of bed.

"Oh, you're back," he said, and maybe it was her imagination, but he didn't seem happy to see her. Maybe he was hurt that she hadn't readily accepted his proposal. Maybe he was angry that she'd taken so long and hadn't been in contact.

"I'm back," she said with a smile that she hoped didn't look as forced as it felt. She thought that maybe seeing him again after such a long time apart would stir up feelings that had been buried or repressed, but she didn't feel a thing. "I thought we could talk."

"Um, well…" He glanced back over his shoulder, into the front room. "Now's not the best time."

She frowned. "Are you sick?"

"No, no, nothing like that."

Liv heard a voice behind him say, "Billy, who is it?"

A *female* voice. Then the door opened wider and a young girl whom Liv didn't recognize stood there dressed in, of all things, one of William's T-shirts.

"Hi!" she said brightly. "Are you a friend of Billy's?"

Billy?

"We work in the lab together," William said, shooting Liv a look that said, *Go along with it.* He obviously didn't want this girl to know that she and William had had anything but a professional relationship. Which, if you wanted to get technical, they never really had.

"I'm Liv," Liv said, because William didn't introduce them. She had the feeling he wished she would just disappear. "And you are?"

The girl smiled brightly. "I'm Angela, Billy's fiancée."

Fiancée? William was *engaged?*

She waved in front of Liv's face a hand sporting an enormous diamond ring. "We're getting married in two weeks," she squealed.

"Congratulations," Liv said, waiting to feel the tiniest bit of remorse, but what she felt instead was relief. She was off the hook. She didn't have to feel bad for turning him down.

"Could you give us a second, Angie?" he said. "It's work."

"Sure," she said, smiling brightly. "Nice to meet you, Liv."

William stepped out onto the porch, closing the door behind him. "I'm so sorry. I wasn't expecting you."

If he'd answered his phone, he would have been, but she was pretty sure they had been otherwise occupied. "It's okay," she said. "I only came here to tell you that I can't marry you."

"Yes, well, when you stopped calling, I just assumed…"

"It just wasn't something I wanted to do over the phone. I guess it doesn't matter now."

"I'm sorry I didn't have a chance to prepare you. I mean, it was very sudden. Obviously."

"I'm very happy for you." And jealous as hell that even he had found someone. Not that he didn't deserve to be happy. It just didn't seem fair that it was so easy for some people. Of course, falling in love with Aaron had been incredibly easy. The hard part was getting him to love her back.

He smiled shyly, something she had never seen him do before, and said, "It was love at first sight."

She left William's house feeling more alone than she had in her entire life. She'd gone from having seven people who accepted her as part of the family—even if the queen had done it grudgingly—to having no one.

Fifteen

Aaron sat in his office, staring out the window at the grey sky through a flurry of snow, unable to concentrate on a single damn thing. He should be down in the greenhouse, meeting with the foreman about the spring crops, but he just couldn't work up the enthusiasm to get his butt out of the chair. The idea of another long season of constantly worrying about growth rates and rainfall and late frosts, not to mention pests and disease, gave him a headache. He was tired of being forced into doing something that deep down he really didn't want to do. He was tired of duty and compromise and putting everyone else's wishes ahead of his own. And even though it had taken a few days for him to admit it to himself, he was tired of shallow, meaningless relationships. He was sick of being alone.

He missed Liv.

Unfortunately she didn't seem to share the sentiment. It had been two weeks since she left and he hadn't heard a word from her. Not even an update on her progress. Yet he couldn't bring himself to pick up the phone and call her. Maybe she'd run back to William.

"Are you going to mope in here all day?"

Aaron looked up to see Anne standing in his office doorway. "I'm working," he lied.

"Of course you are."

He scowled. "Do you need something?"

"I just came by to let you know that I talked to Liv."

He bolted upright in his chair. "What? When?"

"About five minutes ago. She wanted to update us on her progress. And inquire about father's health."

"Why did she call you?"

Anne folded her arms across her chest. "Gosh, I don't know. Maybe because you *broke her heart*."

"Did she say that?"

"Of course not."

"Well," he said, turning toward the window, "she always has William to console her."

"William?"

"He's another scientist. He asked her to marry him before she came here." Not that Aaron believed for a minute she would actually marry William. Not when she admitted she loved Aaron.

"Oh, so *that* was what she meant."

He swiveled back to her. "What?"

"She mentioned that, with the wedding coming up, it might be several weeks before we get another update. I just didn't realize it was *her* wedding."

She was actually going to do it? She was going to compromise and marry a man she didn't love? How could she marry William when she was in love with Aaron?

The thought of her marrying William, or anyone else for that matter, made him feel like punching a hole in the wall. And why? Because he was jealous? Because he didn't like to lose?

The truth hit him with a clarity that was almost painful in its intensity. He loved her. She couldn't marry William because the only man she should be marrying was him.

He rose from his chair and told Anne, "If you'll excuse me, I need to have a word with Mother and Father."

"Something wrong?" Anne said with a grin.

"Quite the opposite." After weeks, maybe even *years* of uncertainty, he finally knew what he had to do.

Aaron found his parents in their suite watching the midday news. "I need to have a word with you."

"Of course," his father said, gesturing him inside.

He picked up the remote and muted the television. "Is there a problem?"

"No. No problem."

"What is it?" his mother asked.

"I just wanted to let you both know that I'm flying to the States today."

"With the Gingerbread Man still on the loose, do you think that's wise?" his father asked.

"I have to see Liv."

"Why?" his mother demanded.

"So I can ask her to marry me."

Her face transformed into an amusing combination of shock and horror. "*Marry* you?"

"That's what I said."

"*Absolutely not.* I won't have it, Aaron."

"It's not up to you, Mother. This is my decision."

"Your father and I know what's best for this family. That girl is—"

"Enough!" his father thundered, causing both Aaron and his mother to jolt with surprise. It had been a long time since he'd been well enough to raise his voice to such a threatening level. "Choose your words carefully, my dear, lest you say something you'll later regret."

She turned to him, eyes wide with surprise. "You're all right with this?"

"Is there a reason I shouldn't be?"

"I know you're fond of her, but a *marriage?* She isn't of noble blood."

"Do you love her, Aaron?" his father asked.

"I do," he said, never feeling so certain of anything in his life.

He turned and asked Aaron's mother, "Do you love our son?"

"What kind of question is that? Of course I do."

"Do you want him to be happy?"

"You know I do. I just—"

"Since Liv has come into his life, have you ever seen him so happy?"

She frowned, as though she didn't like the answer she had to give. "No…but…"

He took her hand. "She's not of noble blood. Who cares? She's a good person. Thoughtful and sweet and kind. If you'd taken any time to get to know her, you would realize that. Royal or not, our son loves her, so she deserves our respect. And our *acceptance*. Life is too short. Shouldn't he spend it with someone who makes him happy? Someone he loves?"

She was silent for a moment as she considered his words, and finally she said, "I want to state for the record that I'm not happy about this."

Aaron nodded. "So noted."

"However, if you love her and she loves you, I suppose I'll just have to learn to accept it."

"You have our blessing," his father told him.

"There's one more thing. I'm going back to school."

His mother frowned. "What for?"

"Because I still need a few science credits before I can apply to med school."

"*Med* school? At your age? What in heaven's name for?"

"Because I've always wanted to."

His father mirrored her look of concern. "But who will oversee the fields?"

"I'm sure we can find someone capable to fill my position. You'll manage just fine without me."

The king didn't look convinced. "Why don't we discuss this when you get back? Maybe we can reach some sort of compromise."

He wanted to tell his father that he was through compromising, but this was a lot to spring on them in one day. It would be best if he gave it some time to sink in.

"All right," he agreed. "We'll talk about it when I get home."

"I want you to take a full security detail with you," his father said. "I know we haven't had any more threats, but I don't want to take any chances."

"Of course," he agreed, and as he left his parents' suite to make the arrangements, he felt an enormous weight had been lifted from his shoulders. That for the first time instead of just watching his life pass by before him, he was finally an active participant. And he knew with a certainty he felt deep in his bones that until he had Liv by his side, life would never be complete.

And he would do anything to get her back.

* * *

It was late in the evening when his limo pulled up in front of Liv's apartment. The building was very plain and unassuming, which didn't surprise him in the least. Hadn't she claimed to spend most of her time in the lab? He hoped she wasn't there now, or, God forbid, at William's place. Not that he wouldn't hunt her down and find her wherever she happened to be. And if William tried to interfere, Aaron might have to hurt him.

Flynn opened the door for him.

"I'm going in alone," Aaron told him.

"Sir—"

"I don't imagine there's an assassin staked out on the off chance that I drop by. You can wait outside."

He nodded grudgingly. "Yes, sir."

Aaron went inside and took the stairs up to the third floor. Her apartment was the first on the right. There was no bell, so he rapped on the door. Only a few seconds passed before it opened, and there stood Liv wearing flannel pajama bottoms and a faded sweatshirt, looking as sweet and sexy and as irresistible as the first time he'd met her.

She blinked several times, as if she thought she might be imagining him there. "Aaron?"

He grinned. "The one and only."

She didn't return his smile. She just looked…confused. In every scenario he had imagined, she had immediately thrown herself into his arms and thanked him for saving her from a life of marital disaster. Maybe this wouldn't be quite as easy as he'd anticipated.

"What are you doing here?" she asked.

"Can I come in?"

She glanced back inside the apartment, then to him, looking uneasy. Had it not occurred to him that William could be there, in her apartment?

"Is someone…*with* you?" he asked.

She shook her head. "No, it's just that my apartment is kind of a mess. I'm getting ready to do some redecorating."

"I won't hold it against you," he said.

She stepped back and gestured him inside. Her apartment was small and sparsely furnished. And what furniture she did have was covered in plastic drop cloths.

"I was getting ready to paint," she explained. She didn't offer to take his coat, or clear a seat for him. "What do you want?"

"I'm here to prevent you from making the worst mistake of your life."

She frowned and looked around the room. "Painting my apartment?"

She looked so hopelessly confused that he had to smile. "No. I'm here to stop you from marrying a man you don't love."

"Why would you think I'm getting married?"

It was his turn to look confused. "Anne said…"

Before he could finish the sentence, reality slapped him in the face. Hard. He'd been set up. Anne was trying to get him off his behind, so he would go after Liv. And he'd given her just the ammunition she needed when he told her about William.

The next time he saw his sister, he was going to give her a big hug.

"I take it you never said anything to my sister about a wedding?"

She shook her head.

"So, you're definitely not marrying William," he confirmed, just to be sure.

"I should hope not, considering he's engaged to someone else."

That was by far the best news Aaron had had all day.

"What difference does it make?" she asked. "Why do you care who I marry?"

"I care," he said, taking a step toward her, "because the only man you should be marrying is me."

Her eyes went wide with disbelief. "I beg your pardon?"

"You heard me." He got down on one knee and pulled the ring box from his coat pocket. He opened it, offering her the five-carat-diamond family ring that sat nestled in a bed of royal-blue velvet. "Will you, Liv?"

For several excruciating seconds that felt like hours, she just stared at him openmouthed, and he began to wonder if she'd changed her mind about him, if, now that they'd been apart for a while, her affection for him had faded. For an instant he genuinely worried that she would actually tell him no.

But when she finally spoke, she said, "You don't want to get married. You're not cut out to be a family man. Remember?"

"Liv, you told me that you love me. Is that still true?"

She bit her lip and nodded.

"And I love you. It took me a while to admit it to myself, but I do. And I couldn't imagine spending the rest of my life with anyone else."

A smile twitched at the corner of her mouth. "What about that excellent rate you get from the girl-of-the-month club?"

He grinned. "I already cancelled my subscription. The only girl I want in my life is you. Now, are you going to make me kneel here all night?"

"But what about your parents? They'll never let you marry a nonroyal."

"They've already given their blessing."

Her eyes went wide. "Your *mother* gave her blessing? Did you have to hold a gun to her head?"

"I'll admit she did it grudgingly, but don't worry, she'll come around. If we give her a grandchild or two, she'll be ecstatic."

"You want that?" she asked. "You really want children?"

"Only if I can have them with you, Liv."

That hint of a smile grew to encompass her entire face. "Ask me again."

He grinned. "Olivia, will you marry me?"

"Yes." She laughed as he slid the ring on her finger, then he pulled her into his arms. "Yes, Your Highness, I definitely will!"

* * * * *

Don't miss Louisa's story available July 2010 from Silhouette Desire.

Celebrate 60 years of pure reading pleasure with Harlequin®!
Just in time for the holidays, Silhouette Special Edition® is proud to present
New York Times *bestselling author*
Kathleen Eagle's
ONE COWBOY, ONE CHRISTMAS.

Rodeo rider Zach Beaudry was a travelin' man—until he broke down in middle-of-nowhere South Dakota during a deep freeze. That's when an angel came to his rescue....

"Don't die on me. Come on, Zel. You know how much I love you, girl. You're all I've got. Don't do this to me here. Not *now*."

But Zelda had quit on him, and Zach Beaudry had no one to blame but himself. He'd taken his sweet time hitting the road, and then miscalculated a shortcut. For all he knew he was a hundred miles from gas. But even if they were sitting next to a pump, the ten dollars he had in his pocket wouldn't get him out of South Dakota, which was not where he wanted to be right now. Not even his beloved pickup truck, Zelda, could get him much of anywhere on fumes. He was sitting out in the cold in the middle of nowhere. And getting colder.

He shifted the pickup into Neutral and pulled hard on the steering wheel, using the downhill slope to get her off the blacktop and into the roadside grass, where she shuddered to a standstill. He stroked the padded dash. "You'll be safe here."

But Zach would not. It was getting dark, and it was already too damn cold for his cowboy ass. Zach's battered body was a barometer, and he was feeling South Dakota, big-time. He'd have given his right arm to be climbing into a hotel hot tub instead of a brutal blast of north wind. The right was his free arm anyway. Damn thing had lost altitude, touched some part of the bull and caused him a scoreless ride last time out.

It wasn't scoring him a ride this night, either. A carload of teenagers whizzed by, topping off the insult by laying on the horn as they passed him. It was at least twenty minutes before another vehicle came along. He stepped out and waved both arms this time, damn near getting himself killed. Whatever happened to *do unto others?* In places like this, decent people didn't leave each other stranded in the cold.

His face was feeling stiff, and he figured he'd better start walking before his toes went numb. He struck out for a distant yard light, the only sign of human habitation in sight. He couldn't tell how distant, but he knew he'd be hurting by the time he got there, and he was counting on some kindly old man to be answering the door. No shame among the lame.

It wasn't like Zach was fresh off the operating table—it had been a few months since his last round of repairs—but he hadn't given himself enough time. He'd lopped a couple of weeks off the near end of the doc's estimated recovery time, rigged up a brace, done some heavy-duty taping and climbed onto another bull. Hung in there for five seconds—four seconds past feeling the pop in his hip and three seconds short of the buzzer.

He could still feel the pain shooting down his leg with every step. Only this time he had to pick the damn thing up, swing it forward and drop it down again on his own.

Pride be damned, he just hoped *somebody* would be answering the door at the end of the road. The light in the front window was a good sign.

The four steps to the covered porch might as well have been four hundred, and he was looking to climb them with a lead weight chained to his left leg. His eyes were just as screwed up as his hip. Big black spots danced around with tiny red flashers, and he couldn't tell what was real and what wasn't. He stumbled over some shrubbery, steadied himself on the porch railing and peered between the vertical slats.

There in the front window stood a spruce tree with a silver star affixed to the top. Zach was pretty sure the red sparks were all in his head, but the white lights twinkling by the hundreds throughout the huge tree, those were real. He wasn't too sure about the woman hanging the shiny balls. Most of her hair was caught up on her head and fastened in a curly clump, but the light captured by the escaped bits crowned her with a golden halo. Her face was a soft shadow, her body a willowy silhouette beneath a long white gown. If this was where the mind ran off to when cold started shutting down the rest of the body, then Zach's final worldly thought was, *This ain't such a bad way to go.*

If she would just turn to the window, he could die looking into the eyes of a Christmas angel.

* * * * *

Could this woman from Zach's past get the lonesome
cowboy to come in from the cold...for good?
Look for
ONE COWBOY, ONE CHRISTMAS
by Kathleen Eagle.
Available December 2009 from
Silhouette Special Edition®.

Copyright © 2009 by Kathleen Eagle

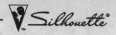

SPECIAL EDITION

We're spotlighting
a different series
every month throughout 2009
to celebrate our 60th anniversary.

This December, Silhouette Special Edition® brings you

NEW YORK TIMES BESTSELLING AUTHOR

KATHLEEN EAGLE

ONE COWBOY, ONE CHRISTMAS

Available wherever books are sold.

Visit Silhouette Books at www.eHarlequin.com

SSE60BPA

Silhouette *Desire*

New York Times Bestselling Author

SUSAN MALLERY

HIGH-POWERED, HOT-BLOODED

Innocently caught up in a corporate scandal, schoolteacher
Annie McCoy has no choice but to take the tempting deal offered
by ruthless CEO Duncan Patrick. Six passionate months later,
Annie realizes Duncan will move on, with or without her. Now
all she has to do is convince him she is the one he really wants!

Available December 2009 wherever you buy books.

ALWAYS POWERFUL, PASSIONATE AND PROVOCATIVE

Visit Silhouette Books at www.eHarlequin.com

SD7698

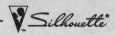

SPECIAL EDITION

**FROM *NEW YORK TIMES* AND *USA TODAY*
BESTSELLING AUTHOR**

KATHLEEN EAGLE

ONE COWBOY,
One Christmas

When bull rider Zach Beaudry appeared
out of thin air on Ann Drexler's ranch,
she thought she was seeing a ghost of
Christmas past. And though Zach had
no memory of their night of passion years
ago, they were about to share a future
he would never forget.

*Available December 2009
wherever books are sold.*

SSE65493

Visit Silhouette Books at www.eHarlequin.com

HQN™

We *are* romance™

New York Times and USA TODAY bestselling author

SUSAN MALLERY

**brings you the final tale
in the Lone Star Sisters series.**

All that stands between Garth Duncan and his goal of taking down his cruel businessman father, Jed Titan, is Deputy Dana Birch, her gun and a growing passion that can't be denied....

Hot on Her Heels

Available now!

www.HQNBooks.com   PHSM38

REQUEST YOUR FREE BOOKS!

2 FREE NOVELS PLUS 2 FREE GIFTS!

Silhouette® *Desire*®

Passionate, Powerful, Provocative!

YES! Please send me 2 FREE Silhouette Desire® novels and my 2 FREE gifts (gifts are worth about $10). After receiving them, if I don't wish to receive any more books, I can return the shipping statement marked "cancel". If I don't cancel, I will receive 6 brand-new novels every month and be billed just $4.05 per book in the U.S. or $4.74 per book in Canada. That's a savings of almost 15% off the cover price! It's quite a bargain! Shipping and handling is just 50¢ per book.* I understand that accepting the 2 free books and gifts places me under no obligation to buy anything. I can always return a shipment and cancel at any time. Even if I never buy another book, the two free books and gifts are mine to keep forever.

225 SDN EYMS   326 SDN EYM4

Name	(PLEASE PRINT)	
Address		Apt. #
City	State/Prov.	Zip/Postal Code

Signature (if under 18, a parent or guardian must sign)

Mail to the Silhouette Reader Service:
IN U.S.A.: P.O. Box 1867, Buffalo, NY 14240-1867
IN CANADA: P.O. Box 609, Fort Erie, Ontario L2A 5X3

Not valid to current subscribers of Silhouette Desire books.

**Want to try two free books from another line?
Call 1-800-873-8635 or visit www.morefreebooks.com.**

Terms and prices subject to change without notice. Prices do not include applicable _es. Sales tax applicable in N.Y. Canadian residents will be charged applicable provincial _es and GST. Offer not valid in Quebec. This offer is limited to one order per household. _orders subject to approval. Credit or debit balances in a customer's account(s) may be _et by any other outstanding balance owed by or to the customer. Please allow 4 to 6 _ks for delivery. Offer available while quantities last.

_ur Privacy: Silhouette Books is committed to protecting your privacy. Our Privacy _icy is available online at www.eHarlequin.com or upon request from the Reader _vice. From time to time we make our lists of customers available to reputable _ parties who may have a product or service of interest to you. If you would _r we not share your name and address, please check here. ☐

SDES09R

COMING NEXT MONTH
Available December 8, 2009

#1981 HIGH-POWERED, HOT-BLOODED—Susan Mallery
Man of the Month
Crowned the country's meanest CEO, he needs a public overhaul.
His solution: a sweet-natured kindergarten teacher who will turn
him into an angel...though he's having a devil of a time keeping
his hands off her!

#1982 THE MAVERICK—Diana Palmer
Long, Tall Texans
Cowboy Harley Fowler is in the midst of mayhem—is seduction
the answer? Don't miss this story of a beloved hero readers have
been waiting to see fall in love!

#1983 LONE STAR SEDUCTION—Day Leclaire
Texas Cattleman's Club: Maverick County Millionaires
He finally has everything he's always wanted within his grasp.
He just can't allow himself to fall for the one woman who nearly
destroyed his empire...no matter how much he still wants her.

#1984 TO TAME HER TYCOON LOVER—Ann Major
Foolishly. she'd given her innocence to the rich boy next door...
only to have her heart broken. Years later, she's vowed not to fall
for his seductive ways again. But she'd forgotten the tycoon's
undeniable magnetism and pure determination.

#1985 MILLIONAIRE UNDER THE MISTLETOE—
Tessa Radley
After unexpectedly sleeping with her family's secret benefactor,
she's taken by surprise when he proposes a more permanent
arrangement—as his wife!

#1986 DEFIANT MISTRESS, RUTHLESS MILLIONAIRE
Yvonne Lindsay
Bent on ruining his father's company, he lures his new assistant
away from the man. But the one thing he never expects is a
double-cross! Will she stick to her mission or fall victim to her
new boss's seduction?